Christmas Traditions at Grace Chapel Inn

Christmas Traditions at Grace Chapel Inn

SUNNI JEFFERS

PAM HANSON & BARBARA ANDREWS

Guideposts
New York, New York

Christmas Traditions at Grace Chapel Inn

ISBN-10: 0-8249-3179-3
ISBN-13: 978-0-8249-3179-7

Published by Guideposts
110 William Street
New York, New York 10038
Guideposts.org

"Jane's Christmas Memory" was written by Sunni Jeffers.

"Louise's Christmas Memory" and "Alice's Christmas Memory" were written by Pam
Hanson and Barbara Andrews.

All Scripture quotations are taken from *The Holy Bible, New International Version*.
Copyright © 1973, 1978, 1984, 2011 by Biblica, Inc. Used by permission of
Zondervan. All rights reserved worldwide. www.zondervan.com

Library of Congress Cataloging-in-Publication Data

Christmas traditions at Grace Chapel Inn.
    p. cm. – (Tales from Grace Chapel Inn)
   Summary: A collection of three novellas celebrating the beauty of Christmas at
Grace Chapel Inn.
    ISBN 978-0-8249-3179-7 (pbk.)
  1. Christmas stories, American. 2. Christian fiction, American.   I. Guideposts
Associates.
    PS648.C43C478 2012
    813′.6–dc23   2012018415

Cover by Deborah Chabrian
Design by Marisa Jackson
Typeset by Aptara, Inc.

Printed and bound in the United States of America
10 9 8 7 6 5 4 3 2

GRACE CHAPEL INN

A place where one can be
refreshed and encouraged,
a place of hope and healing,
a place where God is at home.

*J*ane Howard hummed quietly as she descended the stairs from the third-floor hallway, dimly lit by Victorian wall sconces.

De-dum, de-dum, de-dum, de-dum, on Christmas day, on Christmas day, de-dum, de-dum, de-dum, de-dum, on Christmas day in the morning. She'd pulled her long hair into a ponytail and it bounced against her neck. The fresh, pungent scent of the pine boughs and bayberry draped on the banisters took her back to her childhood, when, as the youngest in the family, she'd crept down the same stairs. Always the first one up on Christmas Day, she would tiptoe to the living room and plug in the Christmas lights, then sit on the floor and gaze at the presents beneath the gaily decorated tree, barely able to contain her excitement.

Christmas was her favorite holiday, when cherished traditions from generations past came alive. Jane loved Christmas even more now that she and her sisters had all moved back home to their family's lovely old Victorian house that they had converted to a bed-and-breakfast called Grace Chapel Inn. They rarely booked guests over Christmas, preferring to celebrate with family and closest friends, and today it would be just Jane and her sisters, plus her niece Cynthia. And, of course, Aunt Ethel, who lived in the carriage house next door.

Family traditions were especially important to Jane because she'd missed so many family connections growing up. Their mother had died when Jane was born and her grandparents had all passed away, so the memories her sisters had shared helped Jane to visualize the attachments she'd missed.

Being first up was part of Jane's normal routine. As a professional chef, she was in charge of breakfasts for the inn, and she started preparations early. Besides, Jane bubbled with energy and a joy for life. She naturally rose early so she wouldn't miss anything.

She peeked into the living room. The room was dark except for the electric candles in the windows, which they always left glowing on Christmas Eve night. She turned on the lights for the Christmas tree in the corner. It sprang to life with sparkling red, green, blue, yellow and white lights. Much better. The stockings hanging on the mantel were filled to overflowing. They were hung in a row by seniority: Aunt Ethel, Louise, Alice, Jane, and Louise's daughter Cynthia.

Jane glanced up on the mantel, where their grandmother's nativity set held center stage. The lovely hand-painted papier-mâché figures were still bright and intact. She looked more closely. The baby Jesus was in the manger. Odd. They always waited until everyone was present to put Jesus there. They would read the nativity story out of the Bible, as their father, the pastor of Grace Chapel, had done. Then one of them would place the baby in the nativity scene. One of her sisters must have gotten up in the middle of the night and completed the nativity.

Shrugging, Jane knelt and started a fire in the fireplace. When it caught, she closed the glass doors. She heard a noise and turned around. Wendell, their gray and black tabby cat, was curled up on his favorite cushioned footstool. He stretched out one white paw and opened one eye to gaze at her.

"Good morning, Wendell. Did you keep watch for Santa last night?" She scratched his head, then headed for the kitchen. He followed, looking for his breakfast.

After she fed the cat, she ground the coffee beans, then started the machine. It dripped and hissed. She turned on the oven, then took a glass casserole dish out of the refrigerator and set it aside to bring it up to room temperature.

She put on a Christmas apron that had been a gift from Louise, pushed the sleeves of her T-shirt up to her elbows, then got out her mother's well-worn recipe book and turned to the Monkey Bread. They were a favorite for special occasions, and a must for Christmas breakfast. She set out flour, sugar, butter, and all the ingredients she needed to start a batter for biscuits. She began humming again, thinking of sleigh bells and glistening snow. Jane rarely sang. She had not inherited her sister Louise's musical talents or her father's clear deep voice, but she loved music and dared to hum when no one was around. The kitchen was her domain, and the sounds of cooking masked her feeble vocal attempts. In her mind, the songs she hummed were lovely. Besides, no one else was awake or could hear her from the upper floors. Kneading dough and humming just seemed to go together.

Louise dried and combed out her short, silvery hair, slipped her glasses and chain over her head to drape around her neck, and put on a soft green merino wool cardigan sweater. In her calf-length gray wool skirt, she was ready for the day. With a spring in her step, she went downstairs. Christmas morning festivities awaited.

The Christmas tree lights were on and a fire danced in the fireplace, warming the room and spreading its cheer. Louise looked out the window. A light dusting of new snow covered the ground. Picture perfect for Christmas Day. She added a log to the fire. As she closed the glass doors and straightened, she noticed the nativity on the mantel. With a twinge of disappointment, she saw the baby Jesus in the manger. Jane must have forgotten to wait until they were all gathered together, as they'd done since they were children. Oh well. It was Christmas morning. She supposed it was all right.

She went down the hall to the kitchen. She heard Jane humming off-key, which grated on Louise's trained ear, but she understood her sister's desire to sing. Music filled the soul. Mentally blocking the sound, she pulled the kitchen door open. Delightful smells burst through the doorway. Cinnamon. Fresh coffee. Vanilla, butter and sugar.

"Yum. It smells divine in here," Louise said. Jane jerked her head around and grinned. The humming stopped.

Jane was in her element. Flour covered the butcher-block countertop and the black-and-white checkerboard floor tiles where she was working. "Good morning. Merry Christmas!"

"Merry Christmas to you too, my dear. Do you need someone to sample something?"

Jane laughed. "Breakfast is a ways out, but I made cherry and almond scone nuggets as appetizers. And the coffee is ready."

"Wonderful. How can I help you?"

"I haven't set the table yet."

"I'll be delighted to do that. But first I'll have some coffee and scones."

"Are we the only ones up?" Jane asked.

"I heard Alice moving around when I passed her door. I don't expect Cynthia to come down until later. She's been working so hard to be able to take this week off, poor darling. She even brought work with her."

"If she isn't down for breakfast, I'll take a tray up to her, but she must come down to open stockings and presents."

Louise chuckled. "I've never known her to be late for that. When she was little, she would come stand at the foot of our bed until either Eliot or I woke up. Then she'd drag us to the living room to start the day."

Jane laughed. "I don't recall ever standing by Father's bed to wake him up, but I got mighty impatient waiting for everyone to come downstairs. I still feel like that little girl sometimes."

"You still *look* like that little girl sometimes. Like now, with syrup on your chin. Have you been licking the bowl?"

"No. I wouldn't do that."

Louise had to laugh at Jane's indignation, which made Jane wave a wooden spoon at her. Jane might be impulsive, and she retained wonderful childlike qualities and youthful cheerfulness, but she was the epitome of professionalism in her kitchen. Licking the bowl was not acceptable in a commercial kitchen.

"Perhaps I'd better see to that table now," Louise said, ducking her head in mock shame and pushing through the swinging door to the dining room.

The Christmas tree lights formed a halo around Louise as she stood staring at the tree, her back to the doorway. When Jane entered the living room, Louise turned around and smiled. "I was just looking at all our ornaments. So many years of memories here."

"Good morning. Merry Christmas!" Alice said, peeking into the room from the doorway. She had on a navy blue pantsuit. Her short, reddish-brown hair had been combed in a neat bob. "Let me get my tea, and I'll join you." She disappeared in the direction of the kitchen.

Jane set her coffee cup on a crocheted doily on the table next to her chair. Alice returned and sat in the rocking chair by the fire. Jane could smell the cinnamon in her special Christmas blend tea. The soft lights bathed the tree ornaments and garlands and the beautiful old decorations in a glow that turned the living room into a magical place. Aunt Ethel and Cynthia would join them soon, but for this moment, the three sisters were together sharing a special time.

Louise walked over and picked up the large brown leather-bound Howard family Bible that had resided on a table in the corner of the living room since Aunt Ethel had given it to the sisters. Though it was only used on special occasions like Christmas morning and Easter, Jane knew the pages that chronicled their family history. On a gold-gilt page with Victorian angels guarding the corners, all of the family births and deaths were listed in the beautiful, flowing script that characterized the lovely penmanship of past generations. Each name had a Bible verse next to it. Jane had added a page with the Berry family history in flowing calligraphy script to match the other entries. The final entry was the date of their father's death.

Louise settled on the couch, put on her glasses, and opened the Bible to the book of Luke. She began reading the familiar words their father had read out loud every Christmas morning.

"And it came to pass in those days, that there went out a decree from Caesar Augustus, that all the world should be taxed. And all went to be taxed, every one into his own city. And Joseph also went up from Galilee, out of the city of Nazareth, into Judaea, unto the city of David, which is called Bethlehem; to be taxed with Mary his espoused wife, being great with child. And so it was, that, while they were there, the days were accomplished that she should be delivered. And she brought forth her firstborn son, and wrapped him in swaddling clothes, and laid him in a manger; because there was no room for them in the inn. And there were—"

"I can do this part," Jane said. Closing her eyes, she recited, "'And there were in the same country shepherds abiding in the field, keeping watch over their flock by night. And, lo, the angel of the Lord came upon them, and the glory of the Lord shone round about them: and they were sore afraid. And the angel said unto them, Fear not, for, behold, I bring you good tidings of great joy, which shall be to all people. For unto you is born this day in the city of David a Savior, which is Christ the Lord. And this shall be a sign unto you; ye shall find the babe wrapped in swaddling clothes, lying in a manger. And suddenly there was with the angel a multitude of the heavenly host praising God, and saying, Glory to God in the highest, and on earth peace, good will toward men.'"

"I remember when you first recited that," Alice said. "What were you, about twelve?"

"At the Bellwood's living Nativity at the farm," Louise said.

"Yes. And I was the angel," Jane said.

"If I remember right, that was the first year Rose and Samuel had the living Nativity out at the farm," Alice said.

"You're correct," Louise said. "They moved there when they got married. And Rose had just had Caleb. He was baby Jesus. That was why I came home to Acorn Hill early, to help Rose so she could be Mary and stay with Caleb all evening in case he needed her."

"He was such a darling baby," Jane said. "Rose let me take care of him while they were building the sets for the nativity. I could really make him giggle."

"I remember that," Alice said. "I wasn't sure about leaving you alone with Caleb. I remember when you'd help in the chapel nursery. You'd carry him around and wouldn't put him down. And with your creativity, who knew what you'd do alone with him."

Louise laughed. "Creativity? That's a nice way to put it."

Jane sniffed. "As I recall, the worst I did was bundle him up and bring him outside—in his buggy—so he could see what everyone was doing."

"So you wouldn't have to miss the action," Alice said.

Jane grinned. "That too. You were having all the fun, pounding nails and painting."

"And freezing our hands off," Alice said.

"I love that they are still doing the live nativity at the farm all these years later," Jane said. "It's the perfect setting, and now their grandchildren are playing parts in it. What a wonderful tradition to pass on to their family and the town. I'm glad I got to play a small part in it."

Alice chuckled. "Yes. A part no one will ever forget."

"Alice! I thought I made a fine angel."

"Fine, and then some," Louise said. "What's the expression Cynthia used the other day? 'Crash-landed and went up in flames?'"

Jane laughed. "I think you mean crashed and burned. And I did not burn."

"But it was a near thing," Alice said. "Scared me half to death."

"I haven't thought of that in years. I didn't want to be an angel, you know. That was Samuel's idea. I wanted to be a shepherd."

"You would have been riding the sheep to see Jesus, not leading them." Alice laughed.

Louise chuckled. "You were quite the tomboy back then."

"I was trying to make it authentic. After all, the Scripture says, 'And, lo, the angel of the Lord came upon them, and the glory of the Lord shone round about them: and they were sore afraid.' They wouldn't have been afraid or surprised if I'd just stood in the loft like you wanted me to. I mean, just imagine if you were outside at night and suddenly an angel appeared in the sky in front of you."

Louise's smile disappeared. "I would be terrified. Awestruck."

"I think so too," Alice said.

"As I recall, I was pretty terrified by your angel, Jane," Louise said. "My first gray hair appeared that year."

"No way," Jane said. "You were only twenty-seven. I do see in hindsight that it could have been a disaster, but everything turned out fine. And I had the best of intentions. I wanted to make an impression, so people would understand the shepherds' surprise. And I wanted to make you and Father proud."

Jane's Christmas Memory

*J*ane peered out the window at the frosty-gray curtain covering the sky that afternoon as Alice drove up the driveway at the Bellwood's farm. Alice parked the Packard sedan in front of the old white Victorian house, and Jane bounced out of the passenger side as soon as Alice turned off the engine. Jane loved visiting the farm. Rose and Samuel treated her like a grown-up, even though she was twelve years younger than Alice. She had to call most adults Mister or Missus or Miss, but not Rose and Samuel. They'd told her to call them by their first names.

Rose let Jane help her in the kitchen and the garden. She'd won first place for her cherry pie at the county fair, and she was teaching Jane how to make a good crust. Sometimes Samuel let her help with the sheep and the other animals around the farm.

Today, Jane was coming to help them build the stage for the Christmas living Nativity they were going to put on at the farm. It seemed like a lot of work to Jane, but if it went well, they talked about doing it every year. Alice had the afternoon off from Potterston Hospital, so she'd picked up Jane from school and driven out here. It was barely three in the afternoon, but the cloudy sky made it dark enough that Samuel had turned on the barn floodlights. As they walked toward the workers, a snowflake landed on Jane's nose. She loved snow. Snow meant sledding on the hill in back of their home. But these flakes disappeared before they hit the ground.

Lloyd Tynan was helping Samuel cut old boards. He was shorter than Samuel, and older. Not as old as her father, but he had to be over thirty, and that, to Jane, was old. And he kept telling Samuel how to do things, as if Samuel didn't know. Jane thought Samuel knew everything about farming and making things. She remembered visiting the farm when he and Rose first moved in, right after they got married. The place was old and run-down, but Samuel fixed everything. The kitchen had been falling apart. He'd torn out the cabinets and made beautiful oak ones with glass doors that showed off Rose's pretty blue and white dishes.

"Hello, Lloyd, Samuel. Jane and I are reporting for duty. Put us to work," Alice said.

The men looked up and smiled. "Great!" Samuel said. "You can brush the dirt off those old boards, then we'll have some painting to do." He looked at Jane for a moment. "You know, you could really help with Caleb if you'd like, so Rose can come out for awhile." Caleb was the Bellwoods' new baby, whom Jane had seen at church several times. "She wanted to come out, but he's sleeping."

"Oh yes, I'd love that. Thanks!" Jane ran to the car and got her school pack, then ran into the house. Jane loved babies. They were so cute and squishy. She tapped on the door, then opened it and walked in, knowing it would be all right. She almost let it slam shut, then remembered the baby was sleeping and put out her foot to keep it from banging. It was warm and moist inside, and she could smell the rich, yeasty scent of something good from the kitchen. She tiptoed in that direction and saw Rose by the sink.

"Hi, Rose," she said in a hushed voice. "I'm here to watch Caleb so you can go outside. Samuel sent me."

Rose turned, and a full smile broke out on her face. "Jane! I'm glad you could come. And that's sweet of you." She took off her apron. "Your timing is perfect. I just took bread out of the oven. I bet you're hungry. Would you like a piece?"

"Oh yes. Thank you."

Steam puffed out as Rose cut a generous slice. She slathered it with fresh churned butter that melted as she spread it and topped it with homemade strawberry jam. She poured a glass of milk to go with the slice and handed them to Jane.

"Caleb is asleep, but he might wake up before too long. There's a diaper and powder on the table. Can you change him all right?"

"Sure. I've done it in the nursery at church." Jane didn't add that she'd had help. Surely she could handle it.

"All right. Yell for me if you need me." Rose put a log in the wood stove so Jane wouldn't need to tend it. She put on a coat and stocking hat and went out through the kitchen door.

Jane gobbled down the bread, then pulled a Nancy Drew book out of her backpack and curled up in an overstuffed chair next to Caleb's cradle.

She'd never noticed how a baby could snore. It was not a loud sound like her father made, but a soft, gentle sighing sound. It reminded Jane of their cat when she purred. Contented. A lovely sound. Distracting at first, but sweet.

The story drew Jane in, and the baby's breathing faded until she didn't hear it anymore. Just as Nancy Drew was escaping out a window, Caleb let out a cry. Jane nearly jumped, then laughed at herself. She wasn't used to babies. She set the book down and leaned over the cradle.

"What's the matter, Caleb?"

He blinked and turned his head toward the sound. His little fist jerked in the air. He inhaled a shaky breath, then let out a wail.

"Hey Caleb, don't cry. I'm here." Jane picked him up and held him against her shoulder, patting him on the back. He let out a big, wet burp.

"Oh my." Jane grabbed the burp cloth that was draped over the end of the cradle and dabbed at his mouth and her shoulder, then tossed the cloth over her shoulder and tucked it under his chest. "There. That should take care of it," she said, looking down at the baby. He looked back with big brown eyes like his mother's. Then he smiled. Jane smiled back. "You're such a pretty boy." His head bobbed like he was agreeing, but Jane knew he was unsteady. After all, he was only three months old.

She laid him on the top of a side dresser that Rose had covered with a blanket to make a changing table. A stack of neatly folded diapers was set on the side. Jane unsnapped the one-piece terry cloth footed pajamas and pulled his little feet out, tickling them and clapping them together to make him laugh. He cooed and let out a gurgling giggle that delighted her. Then his feet and hands started pumping the air and he made little grunting sounds.

"Okay, hold still." She pulled off the one-piece plastic diaper cover, then undid the large diaper pins. Getting it all off was easy. Getting it back on proved a bit harder. He kept wiggling. She put her fingers between the new diaper and his skin, like Mrs. Simpson had shown her in the church nursery. The pins didn't want to go through and she was afraid to push too hard. She didn't want to poke the baby. She worked the tip of the pin until it finally slid through the multiple layers of diaper. As she leaned over him, concentrating on pulling the diaper tight and sticking the other pin through, Caleb reached up and grabbed her hair.

"Ouch. You're so strong," she said. Just then the pin pushed through and jabbed her finger. "*Ee-ouch!*"

At her yell, Caleb's face scrunched up and he started crying. "Oh no, don't cry. It's all right," she said, but he didn't stop. She finished pinning and pulled her hand out. Her finger had a bright red spot on it. She dabbed it on the outside of the diaper, then hoped Rose wouldn't think it was the baby's blood. She managed to get his rubber pants on and tucked his feet back into his pajamas.

"There, there," she said, picking him up and lifting him to her shoulder, patting his back. He finally stopped crying.

"Much better." Jane carried him over to the window, where they could look out. It was darker now, but the light illuminated the workers by the barn. Samuel had built a fire in an old metal barrel. Sparks were dancing in the air. She could hear laughter.

"You want to go see what your mommy and daddy are doing?" Jane asked Caleb. He gurgled. She laughed. "Sure you do. Let's see if we can find you something warm to wrap you up in."

In the dresser drawer, she found a knitted one-piece suit with a hood and feet and hand covers. She bundled Caleb into it. With the hood up, all she could see was his face. She wrapped him in a blanket and placed him in his buggy, which was parked on the enclosed back porch.

"Okay, let's go see what the big people are doing." Jane put on her coat and gloves, then pushed the buggy out the door and across the yard.

"Well, look who we have here," Samuel said. He came over to the buggy and peered in. Caleb started cooing. Samuel brushed off his hands and reached in, pulling his son out and lifting him up to his shoulder. His hands were so big they nearly encompassed the baby. "Hey buddy, did you come to help us build this contraption?" Samuel said in his deep voice. He chuckled when Caleb bobbed his head and drooled all over his father's shoulder.

"I guess he isn't too keen on your idea," Lloyd said, chuckling.

"Guess not." Samuel grinned and handed Caleb to Rose, who reached out for him.

"I bet he's hungry. I'll go inside and feed him."

"I changed him, so he's dry," Jane said.

"Great. Thank you, Jane." Rose took Caleb and carried him inside, leaving the buggy outside. Jane was struck by how large he looked on his mother's shoulder. When Samuel held him, he looked tiny. But Rose was petite and Samuel was a giant.

Jane turned to Samuel. "Can I help?"

"We're finishing up for the night. It's getting too dark to work. You can help us move everything into the barn. We'll work again Saturday afternoon."

"Can we come back, Alice?"

"We'll see. I need to help with the flowers at the chapel. Then if Father doesn't need us, perhaps we can come."

"Okay." Jane picked up a board and carried it into the barn and stacked it with the others Lloyd had stashed inside an empty stall. In the next stall, a litter of kittens made tiny mewling sounds. The mama cat was gone. "Can I go see the kittens?" Jane asked.

"Yes. They're two weeks old. Their eyes are just opened. They can't really see, but you can pick them up if you're very gentle," Samuel said.

"I will be," Jane said, opening the stall gate and going inside. Five kittens were in a box that was nestled in the hay. Jane picked up a tan and white kitten. Cradling it in the palm of her hand, she held it up close to her face. "Aren't you a cutie. So soft. You remind me of the fur muff that belonged to my grandma. I'm going to call you Muffy." She nuzzled the tiny kitten. It stared at her. Samuel said it couldn't see her, but it seemed to be looking right into her eyes.

The mama cat jumped into the box and let out a meow, letting Jane know she missed her baby. "Hello, Bella," Jane said, setting the kitten in the box and scratching the mama's head. She'd spent many afternoons holding and petting the gray and white cat.

Bella blinked her eyes, then started bathing the kitten with her tongue, ignoring Jane.

"Don't feel bad," Samuel said. "She ignores all of us now that she has babies."

"Oh, it's all right. I don't blame her." Jane looked around. Puddin', the black-and-white milk cow, was eating her dinner of hay and grain in one stall. Their yearling donkey was rubbing his head against the rails in another stall. Jane went over and climbed the rail gate and reached to scratch his head. He came over and nearly knocked her off her perch.

Jane laughed. "Whoa. Easy, Pesky. There. Does that feel good?" she asked, rubbing around his ears. He kept pushing against her hands.

Samuel dropped a couple of flakes of hay into his stall. Pesky turned away and started munching the hay.

"Samuel, can I be a shepherd in the nativity?"

"Well. . ." Samuel leaned on his pitchfork and scratched his chin. "You'd make a good shepherd, but I had something else in mind. Something only you could do."

Jane's shoulders slumped. She wanted to be with the animals. She was good with them. "Oh." She peered up at him, her eyes imploring him to change his mind.

"I was hoping you could be the angel who announces the baby Jesus. The angel is going to stand way up in the hayloft, so we need someone agile enough to go up in the barn loft, who isn't afraid of heights, and who can recite the angel's lines. I think you'd be perfect."

She could see that he thought she'd be pleased by the offer. And most of the girls her age probably would consider it the best part, since you probably got to wear a fancy costume. But it sounded boring to Jane. She would much rather be playing with the animals on the ground.

Still, she couldn't turn down Samuel. He was always so nice to her. And when she thought about it, she couldn't imagine any-one else going up to the loft to be the angel. Alice always com-pared Jane to a monkey because of her tree-climbing skills. And Jane had to admit, she was pretty agile.

"Sure. I'll be happy to be the angel," she said, and gave Samuel a smile, although she was not thrilled. An angel. Alice would laugh about that.

Samuel smiled and looked relieved. "Let's go inside and see if Rose has some hot chocolate made."

"Oh yeah!"

Samuel carried the pitchfork to a peg by the big sliding barn door and hung it up. Jane followed him. They went out and Samuel slid the big door shut. He handled it like it was light-weight, but Jane knew better. It was a huge door with wheels at the top that ran along a rail. Jane could barely make it budge. Once it started rolling, it closed all right, though.

Alice and Lloyd were already in the kitchen sipping big mugs of hot chocolate and eating oatmeal raisin cookies.

"Rose is putting the baby down upstairs," Alice said. "The cocoa should still be hot."

Samuel got two mugs and filled one for Jane. He went to the refrigerator and took out a bowl of whipped cream. "You do want cream on yours, don't you?"

"Of course! Thanks." Jane sat at the table and took a cookie. She took a big sip of the cocoa that Samuel set in front of her. She licked the whipped cream mustache from her upper lip. "*Mmm.* Good. Guess what, Alice? I'm going to be the angel in the nativity."

"That's wonderful." She looked at Samuel, then back at her. "You're perfect for the part."

"Really? You think so?"

"Yes, I do."

Jane nodded and took a big sip of her cocoa. If Alice thought she could do it, then it would be all right.

"*Ouch!*" Jane tried to jerk her head away. That was a mistake. It hurt even worse.

"Sorry. But don't pull." Alice eased her grip on Jane's hair. "I'm almost finished." Alice wrapped a rubber band around Jane's pigtail. "There. Do you want ribbons?"

"No. I'm too big for ribbons. And do I have to wear a skirt?"

"Yes. I'm not wild about it either, but Florence— Mrs. Simpson—is very particular."

Jane scrunched her nose. "Do we have to go? I don't even like to do crafts."

"She's part of the church. As the pastor's daughters, we have a responsibility to support and encourage all the members."

"She doesn't–" Jane stopped short, remembering her father's reproach to her the day before when she complained about a teacher. "He that shutteth his lips is esteemed a man of understanding" (Proverbs 17:28, KJV). It was a verse their father quoted often. Alice had explained that verse to her many years ago. If you can't say something nice about someone, don't say anything at all. Their father would not allow gossip or unkind words. He rarely punished Jane, but his disapproval hurt her far more than if he would send her to her room or make her miss dessert.

"Mrs. Simpson is doing this as a treat for the ladies of the church. And she specifically invited you to attend with me."

"But you don't do crafts either, Alice."

"I might make a gift for Aunt Ethel or Louise," Alice said. "Maybe you can make one too. And I'm sure Florence will serve lots of Christmas cookies. She was busy baking last week."

Jane sighed. "All right. We don't have to stay very long, do we?"

Alice pulled the brush through Jane's hair. "Not too long. Ready?"

"I guess. What's that?"

Alice had picked up a paper bag. "We're supposed to take craft supplies to share. I had no idea what to take. I ran into Clarissa Cottrell at the General Store. She does lots of crafts, and she helped me pick out some materials. We need to take scissors too."

"Oh. What can we make with this stuff?" Jane asked, peering into the bag.

"I'm not sure." Alice started toward the door, gesturing for Jane to follow her. "But Clarissa said she will be there, so she can show us. Put on your coat."

Jane did as she was told, though she moved slowly.

"Good-bye, Father. We'll be back in time to prepare dinner," Alice said as they passed their father's study. He was working on his sermon for Sunday.

"Have a nice time," he said, glancing at them over his glasses.

Jane went into the study and gave him a hug and a kiss. He gave her a hug and a peck on her cheek. Jane adored her quiet, studious father. He never raised his voice at her, even though she knew she was sometimes overly enthusiastic. She'd overheard Florence Simpson tell several ladies at church that someone should tell Rev. Howard that his youngest daughter needed discipline and boundaries. The ladies didn't know she was outside the door, and she'd snuck away.

That conversation had bothered her for days. She never told her sister or her father, but she had avoided Mrs. Simpson and the other ladies after that, afraid she would slip up. She never meant to cause trouble. But sometimes it just happened. The thought of going to the Simpson's house made her nervous. She supposed she'd have to face Mrs. Simpson eventually. She would try to be on her best behavior. After all, as one of the ladies had pointed out, her behavior reflected on her father and his ministry. She did not want to disappoint her father or cause anyone to think less of him because of her.

⤬

"Jane."

Jane heard the loud whisper and looked over at the formal living room of the Simpson home. It was a grand home, larger than the Howard home, which was a substantial Victorian. The Simpsons lived in a brick mansion filled with beautiful paintings in heavy, gilded frames and delicate statues and china. Jane was almost afraid to move because she might accidentally bump into something and break it. Tables were set up in the room and Jane recognized the ladies who were chatting and drinking tea, but no one was looking at her.

"Your coat, please." Ronald Simpson, Florence's husband, was playing butler for his wife's party. He held a wooden hanger in one hand and reached out for her coat with the other.

"Oh. Thank you." As she removed her coat and handed it to him, she heard her name again.

"Jane. Over here."

She turned and smiled with relief when she saw her school friend Doreen waving to her from a table in the parlor across from the living room. At least she wasn't the only girl there. And there was an empty seat next to her.

"Alice, can we go in the parlor?"

Alice looked in that direction. "I told Clarissa—oh, she's in there too. Certainly." Alice gave Ronald her coat and they went into the parlor. Clarissa Cottrell was at the same table with Doreen and her mother. There were two empty chairs, so Alice sat next to Clarissa, and Jane sat next to her friend Doreen. The tables were neatly covered with butcher paper.

"I was starting to worry," Doreen whispered, leaning close to Jane. "I only came because I heard you were coming."

"I was afraid I'd be the only girl here," Jane whispered back.

"Welcome to my home, ladies," Florence said from the hallway, facing the living room, then turning to the parlor. "I'm so glad you could come. I've arranged the dining room for all the craft supplies, so if you will bring your offerings, I'll explain more in that room. Leave your scissors and other tools at your place." She turned and walked down the hall.

They had just sat down, but everyone got up from their seats and followed her down the hall, as instructed. About twenty ladies crowded around the large dining room table. Jane and Doreen were at the back. They stood on tiptoes, trying to see, but they were just too short.

"Come over here, girls," Rose Bellwood said. She was petite— not much taller than Jane. She stood over on the far end of the room. They made their way to her side, and they could see the foot of the table and Florence, who stood behind it.

Various sizes of bowls for the craft supplies were set out on the table. Alice handed Florence their sack of craft supplies, and Florence poured the glitter into one bowl and the sequins into another, and then set the fabric on one end of the table with the other fabrics. Florence held up a beaded star she'd laid out on the table. "Here is one example of a Christmas craft. There are several other finished crafts here that you can look at too. Copies of the instructions are here."

She pointed to a stack of papers on the edge of the table. "You can take a plate and put what you need for your craft on it, then take it to your table."

She turned toward Jane and Doreen. "And girls, please be careful you don't spill anything on the floor. The Oriental carpets are quite expensive."

Jane blushed, but nodded. She knew those instructions were aimed at her. Why had Alice made her come?

Jane waited until the ladies had taken their supplies. Then she approached the table. Most of the crafts were Christmas tree ornaments. A beaded star, a wreath, and a tree. A decorated canning jar to hold a candle. Braided ribbons made into a cluster of colorful loops. A felt gingerbread man and a snowman. A felt-covered cone ornament decorated with sequins.

Jane couldn't decide. What would Louise like?

"What are you going to make, Jane?" Clarissa Cottrell asked as she picked up a strand of gold ribbon.

Jane liked Clarissa. She was older, like Florence Simpson, but she seemed younger than that. She worked with her mother and father at the Good Apple Bakery. She always talked to Jane and asked her about school, and sometimes she gave Jane an extra cookie.

"I don't know. I want to make something for Louise. She likes old-fashioned things."

"How about the cone? You could fill it with candy."

"Maybe." Jane studied the offerings on the table. "But it looks kind of ordinary."

"I agree. But you don't have to make it out of felt. You could cut it out of the interfacing Alice brought."

Jane nodded. So that was what that white stuff Alice brought was.

"That would make it stiff," Clarissa explained. "Then you could cover it with pretty fabric."

"*Hmm.*" There was red and green material and fabric with poinsettias on it. Then Jane spotted squares of silver satin lamé fabric. "Maybe I could."

Jane looked over the supplies and spotted a bowl filled with tiny, wispy white feathers. That gave her an idea. She picked up a square of the fabric and a pattern piece for the cone. Clarissa showed her how to pin the pattern onto the heavy interfacing fabric. Jane followed her instructions and cut out a triangle. She would roll it up to make a cone. Then she took a piece of thin green satin ribbon, some sequins, and a pile of the feathers and carried them back to the table.

Doreen was already back in her seat, stringing colored beads onto wire. Jane set her supplies on the table and picked up the glue. Rolling the cut triangular shape into a cone, she overlapped the edges and glued them, then held them in place while the glue dried. Some of the glue dripped onto the butcher paper. Jane wiped it with her finger, then looked for something to clean it off her finger. There was nothing around, so she wiped it on the back of the silver lamé.

When she laid out the fabric and cut it to match the pattern, it got a little of the glue on the front. She dabbed at it, then smeared glue on the back and shaped it over the cone. Then, using the tip of the scissors, she poked a hole on each side of the top and strung the ribbon through for a hanger, tying it together in a bow.

"That's taking shape nicely," Clarissa said from across the table.

"That's pretty neat," Doreen said. "Better than my beads, although I like the way they shine in the light." She held up the ornament she'd shaped into a star.

"That's pretty," Jane said. She ran a line of glue around the open top of her cone and carefully glued the feathers in place along the rim. Holding it up, eyeing it critically, she could see where dots of glue marred the fabric.

"Does anyone know how to draw one of those curlicues on music?" she asked.

"Do you mean a treble clef?" Doreen's mother asked.

"I think so. Like on piano music."

"Yes. It looks like a backward *S* with a line down through it, like this." She drew it on a napkin and handed it to Jane.

"That's it! Thanks." Jane sketched one on the side of the cone, then glued sequins along the lines.

"Jane, that's beautiful," Alice said.

"Do you think so? Do you think Louise will like it?"

"Like it? She'll love it," Clarissa said. "I didn't know you were so artistic."

Jane smiled, pleased. It was pretty. Maybe craft parties weren't so bad after all.

"Since you girls are finished, clean up your place and you can get some cookies and punch," Doreen's mother said.

"All right!" Doreen said.

The girls cleaned up and threw away their scraps, then took their extra supplies back to the dining room. Plates of beautiful cookies and candies and a cut crystal punch bowl were set on the sideboard.

There was a stack of lovely cream-colored dessert plates with gold rims and cut crystal glasses for the punch. Doreen filled a plate with a sample of everything and headed back to their table. Jane remembered Alice's warning not to take everything, but to leave enough for everyone else, so she studied the table, trying to decide which ones to choose. They all looked delicious. She had picked a frosted, decorated sugar cookie and a piece of divinity fudge and was deciding what else to take when she heard Alice in the hallway.

"This was a lovely party, Florence," she said.

"Thank you. I do love to entertain, you know. And I feel it's my duty to share the blessings Ronald and I have received from the Lord."

"Yes, that is very generous," Alice replied.

"I understand Samuel Bellwood has appointed Jane to be the herald angel for the living Nativity," Florence said. "Is that correct?"

Jane's hand stilled, inches from the petits fours, frozen in place as she listened. Mrs. Simpson never said anything good about her.

"Yes, and she will be a wonderful angel," Alice said. "We're already trying to figure out a costume for her."

"*Humph*. You are optimistic. Mark my words, that girl will find some way to disrupt the nativity."

"No, Florence." Jane could hear that Alice was struggling to hide her frustration. "Jane has a sweet nature and a kind heart. She is suited to this part, and she will announce Christ's birth in true angelic fashion."

Jane let out the breath she'd been holding and hoped Alice was right. She did tend to be exuberant on occasion, as she'd heard her father say. She never meant to create a stir, but it happened. Bless Alice for defending her.

As Jane put a petit four on her plate, Alice and Florence walked into the dining room.

"Hello, dear," Alice said, giving Florence a frown, then smiling at Jane.

Jane was glad she hadn't piled her plate high. Mrs. Simpson had to know she'd heard them talking. She tried to think of something to say. She smiled. "These cookies are lovely, Mrs. Simpson. You sure are a good cook."

"Thank you, Jane. Do try a fruit tart."

"Oh, thank you." She used the small gold tongs to pick up a tartlet and place it on her plate. She took a glass of punch that had already been poured and returned to the parlor, glad to escape.

As lovely and delicious as the treats looked, Jane had lost her appetite. She ate them because it wasn't polite to leave food on her plate, but all she wanted was to leave.

Alice must have sensed her discomfort. She thanked the Simpsons and said good-bye. In a few moments they were climbing into Alice's old blue and white, two-door Packard.

"I'm so sorry you overheard Mrs. Simpson, Jane. She can be critical, but she means well."

Jane stared ahead out the window and nodded. "She doesn't like me."

"Oh, I don't think that's true. You know people are hardest on the ones they love."

"She doesn't love me. She thinks I'm an embarrassment to Father." Jane felt tears well up in her eyes. She tried to focus on the houses, decorated with holly and evergreens, as they drove through town. "And sometimes she's right."

"Oh, honey, you never embarrass Father or me or anyone else. Don't believe that."

Alice pursed her lips together. She looked angry. At Jane? Or at Mrs. Simpson? Jane didn't know, but she didn't want her sister upset. "I'm sorry. I don't mean to get into trouble."

Alice looked at Jane and smiled. "Did I ever tell you I was a tomboy too?"

"Louise told me you were, but I can't believe it."

"Well, I was. And Florence Simpson used to snap at me and tell me to act like a lady. And she's only four years older than I am. Don't take it to heart. She had a strict upbringing, and she can't help it."

"I don't embarrass you?"

"No. Never." Alice flipped on her turn signal and slowed at a stop sign. Then she eased the car right onto Chapel Road. "Worry me? Now that's different. When I see you standing on a limb at the top of the maple tree, I can't help but have a bit of concern."

"Oh." Jane sighed and relaxed back against the seat. "That's all right, then."

Alice laughed.

Jane held her arms out to her sides, trying to stand still. Alice worked on one side and Rose worked on the other, pinning the heavy white fabric under her arms and down her sides. She was standing on a stool in the middle of the spare bedroom at the Bellwoods' house.

"This looks like my bedspread, only white instead of pink," Jane said.

"Hold still so I don't poke you," Alice said.

"It is, or was, a bedspread," Rose said. "It was in a trunk in the attic when we moved into the farm. It's chenille. Perfect for an angel's robes. And it will be warm."

"Oh." Rose had cut the cloth so that long pieces of fabric hung down from the arms like wings. Jane wanted to move her arms up and down as if she were flying. She resisted, waiting patiently for Alice to finish.

"Will I have wings?"

"Yes. Samuel is making a frame out of wire. I'm not sure how we'll attach them to you, but we'll figure it out," Rose said.

"Turn around Jane. I need to pin the hem in the back," Alice said.

Jane turned. She could see baby Caleb lying on a quilt on the floor, his chubby little arms and legs pumping the air. He was cooing and gurgling. Jane laughed. He stopped for a few seconds and seemed to be looking around. Then he started again. She was certain he'd heard her laugh and recognized her. He was so adorable.

"That's good for now. Let's slip it over your head," Rose said.

Jane reached down and started to pull it off.

"Whoa. Wait," Alice said. "You'll pull the pins out, or get stuck. Let me help you."

Rose and Alice carefully pulled the pinned robe over Jane's head and off of her arms.

"You did well, Jane. I know it's hard to stand still for so long. That deserves a cup of tea and a scone. I made some fresh this morning. Let's go in the kitchen." Rose picked up Caleb and his quilt and went downstairs. She put him in his cradle next to the kitchen table.

Jane sat close to the cradle, where she could see Caleb. When she leaned over the cradle and talked gibberish to him, his face broke into a big, toothless smile and he gurgled a happy sound. She tickled his tummy and he giggled and squealed. Jane loved playing with Caleb and drinking tea in Rose's kitchen. She didn't like standing on a stool, holding still for what seemed like an hour, but this made it all worth it.

"Louie!" Jane ran to the kitchen door and hugged her big sister Louise, who was fifteen years older than she was. Louise lived in Philadelphia with her new husband, and she didn't come home nearly enough for Jane's taste. She had come home for Christmas a week early to help Rose and Samuel with the living Nativity. Louise looked fashionable in a black curly lambs wool coat and matching hat with velvet trim. "I'm so glad you're here early!" Jane took her hand to pull her into the kitchen.

"Hello, Jane. My, you've grown! We're almost eye-to-eye. What have you been eating? Some kind of magic beans?"

Jane stood to her full height and laughed. "No, silly. Father says I've had a growth spurt."

"Indeed you have," a deep voice said from the doorway.

"Eliot!" Jane hugged her brother-in-law, though with a bit more restraint. He was a reserved man, and it made her pause to think of him as her brother, since he was so old. Fifteen years older than Louise. To Jane, he seemed almost as old as her father. But he fit with Louise, who was very serious and motherly, and he treated Jane with kindness and affection.

"Hello, Jane. I brought you a present." He pulled a Hershey bar from his suit pocket.

"Oh, thank you!" With her usual impulsiveness, Jane bounced up and kissed Eliot on the cheek, the way she would her father or Uncle Bob. He blushed.

"Louise, dear, shall I carry our luggage up to your old room?"

"It's all ready for you," Alice said, coming into the kitchen. She hugged Louise, then Eliot. "Dinner will be in an hour. Go get settled and refreshed."

"We will, as soon as we greet Father. Is he in his study?"

"Yes. Would you like to take him his tea?"

"I would." Louise removed her hat and gloves and hung her coat on a hook by the back door.

Jane adored her oldest sister and her husband. They were so sophisticated. Jane supposed that was because they lived in a big city. Eliot was a music professor at a college and Louise played and taught piano. Jane had no desire to learn the piano, but she loved to hear her sister play. Now that they were home, their house would be filled with Christmas music on the old piano in the parlor.

When they came down for dinner, Louise had changed into a more casual wool skirt and sweater. Eliot still wore his wool dress pants with turned-up cuffs, but he'd exchanged his wool blazer for a sweater vest. Jane was secretly glad she lived in Acorn Hill, where she could wear pants, except for school and church. Alice disliked skirts too, so Jane had a champion there.

They ate dinner in the dining room on the heirloom blue and white Wedgwood china that had belonged to their grandmother. They usually ate at the kitchen table on a set of dishes with red and yellow roses, but tonight was a special occasion because Louise and Eliot were there. Alice had cooked pot roast and all the trimmings, one of Jane's favorite meals. Jane had helped peel the potatoes and carrots.

Their father prayed before the meal, thanking God for Eliot and Louise's safe travel and for the bounty of their blessings.

Jane sat patiently while the bowls of food were passed, but inside she was bouncing in her chair. Not for the food. Finally she couldn't stand it.

"Louise, I made your Christmas present," she announced.

Louise stopped, holding a large spoonful of mashed potatoes in midair. She deposited the food on her plate and handed the serving bowl to her father, then turned her attention to Jane, one eyebrow raised.

"Really? I cannot wait to see it. Will you give me a hint?"

"Oh no. I can't do that. But it's all shiny and it has a surprise in it."

"*Hmm.* I can't imagine. Oh dear, and now I must wait to open it."

"Yes, and no peeking. I wrapped it and hid it in my room."

Louise's smile held mischief. "Now I am tempted. You can't guard your room all the time."

"Oh no! Promise you won't go in there," Jane said, a bit alarmed. She couldn't imagine her big sister tearing her room apart looking for the present, but she had tempted her. She couldn't lock the door. The big skeleton key hanging in the kitchen by the back door opened every lock in the house.

Louise placed a finger on her chin and frowned for a moment. "What if I want to help you clean your room?"

Jane thought for a moment. Having her sister help her clean was tempting. But then she'd have an excuse to go in while Jane was at school. Christmas vacation didn't start for a week. "I can keep it clean by myself," Jane said, unwilling to take a chance.

"Or I might need to get your dirty clothes for the laundry."

This was getting serious. "I'll bring my dirty clothes downstairs."

"Well, then, I suppose I won't have a reason to go in your room. All right. I promise."

Louise didn't smile. She seemed serious, yet Jane thought she detected a twinkle in her eyes. But she promised, so that was good enough. The surprise was safe until Christmas morning, or maybe Christmas Eve. Jane relaxed and accepted the gravy pitcher that Alice passed to her. She poured hot gravy over everything on her plate—meat, potatoes, cooked carrots, and onions and turnips.

"No wonder you're having a growth spurt," Louise said, chuckling. "I think I'll call you Sprout. You are sprouting up. Keep it up and you'll be taller than I am."

"I'd like that," Jane said, shoveling a spoonful of potato in her mouth. "Then I can have your hand-me-downs."

Louise laughed. "By that time, my clothes will be out of fashion."

"Oh. I didn't think of that."

"Eliot, are you able to stay for a chess match tomorrow? The board is set up in the library," Father said.

Eliot shook his head. "Much as I would love to, I must return to Philadelphia tomorrow after lunch. I have exams to give before Christmas break. But I'll take a rain check. We'll have time for several matches when I come for Christmas."

"Eliot, will you be back in time for the living Nativity?" Jane asked. "I'm going to be the angel."

"That's wonderful," Louise said.

"And a fine angel you'll be," her father said.

"Alice and Rose are making my costume. I'm going to have wings and everything."

"Will you have a halo?" Eliot asked.

"I don't know. Will I, Alice?"

"I believe Samuel is working on that."

"Neat-o. But Mrs. Simpson thinks I shouldn't be the angel. She thinks I'll ruin the nativity."

Father frowned. "Don't be concerned about what Mrs. Simpson said, Jane. Sometimes she voices her thoughts out loud. That doesn't mean she is right. I believe you are the perfect person to play the angel. You have enthusiasm and a pure heart. Imagine how excited the angels must have been to announce the news that God's Son was coming to mankind to be born as a human. I can't see anyone else playing that part. Have you learned your lines?"

"Most of them."

"We'll work on them next week after school," Louise said. "I'll have plenty of time to help you."

"That'd be great," Jane said. Although she wasn't too keen on memorizing lines, she knew she had to learn them. She wanted to prove that Mrs. Simpson and the other ladies were wrong about her, and she wanted to make her father and sisters, and Samuel and Rose, truly proud.

"*Yoo-hoo!* Anybody here?" Aunt Ethel entered the kitchen the next day after church. Her husband Bob was right behind her carrying a box.

"Aunt Ethel!" Jane rushed forward ahead of Louise and hugged their aunt around her middle, nearly knocking her backward into Uncle Bob.

"*Whoa.* Hello, Jane." She hugged her young niece back.

"Where's Francie?"

"Francine had a birthday party to attend and the boys are visiting friends. We dropped them off and thought we'd stop by to see Louise and Eliot."

"Oh." Jane looked disappointed. She let go of their aunt and stepped back. Her cousin Francine was her age, the youngest of Aunt Ethel and Uncle Bob's children. Ethel was their father's half-sister. Ethel and Bob lived on a farm outside Acorn Hill. They often stopped to visit when they were in town. Louise and her sisters had spent many wonderful afternoons at the Buckley farm.

"Aunt Ethel. Uncle Bob. So nice to see you," Louise said, hugging each of them. "We're just about ready for Sunday dinner. Won't you join us?"

"We don't want to put you to any trouble," Ethel said. "We just wanted to say hi." She took off her gloves and set her purse on the counter.

"We have plenty of food."

Ethel looked at Bob. He just smiled. "Sure, we'll be happy to join you," she said, removing her coat. She was wearing a stylish red and blue paisley, long-sleeved A-line dress, which set off her bouffant carrot-red hair and blue clip-on earrings and matching necklace.

"Eliot and Father are in the living room, if you'd like to join them, Uncle Bob. Dinner won't be ready for a few minutes."

Bob took Ethel's coat and hung it with his on a hook by the door. Then he left the ladies to go join the men.

Ethel took a seat at the kitchen table, crossed her legs, and straightened her skirt, then looked up at Louise. "So tell me how you've been. You are looking fine. I was surprised when Alice said you were coming this weekend. I didn't expect you for at least another week. Are you staying through Christmas and New Year's?" Ethel finally ran out of questions and stopped, looking at Louise expectantly.

"We're doing fine. I came early to help get ready for Christmas. Eliot has to return to the city this afternoon, but he'll be back when classes let out."

Alice came into the kitchen from the dining room. "Hello, Aunt Ethel. I heard you were here, so I set places for you at the table. How have you been?"

"Oh, you know. Busy as usual," she said, waving one hand dismissively. "I was in charge of the Christmas bake sale and Santa's visit at the Grange Hall yesterday. It turned out to be the best Christmas event in many years. They've already asked me to head the event again next year." She held up her hand as if examining her shiny red fingernails.

"That's wonderful. You're so good at organizing things. And I always loved your Christmas cookies," Louise said.

"I'll be sure to bake an extra batch to bring for all of you to share. I know it's difficult without your dear mother here to make Christmas special."

"Yes, it is. That's one reason I wanted to come early. Alice is so busy working, she doesn't have much time. I can help decorate and bake and make sure we celebrate with some of Mother's favorite traditions to make the holidays more memorable.

When Jane arrived home from school Monday afternoon, she found Louise and Father in the living room. Father was on a step-ladder, holding a tree, while Louise stood back to make sure it was straight. A long string of Christmas lights was draped over the couch and chairs and across the floor. She had to step over them. There were boxes all over the floor.

"You got a Christmas tree!"

"Yes. Father and I went out to Bellwood Farm and they let us cut one in their woods."

The tree nearly reached the tall ceiling in the corner of the living room. Their mother's rocking chair had been moved closer to the fireplace to make room for the tree.

"That looks straight. Hold it while I tighten the base," Louise said. She got down on her hands and knees and reached under the tree. "We'll have to snip off some of these low branches to make room for gifts," she said. She backed out and stood. "There. Let go and let's see if it holds."

Father released his grip, but stayed on the ladder to make sure the tree wouldn't tilt or fall. It held in place. "Hand me a string of lights, Louise."

Louise unplugged one strand from the next and handed it up to her father. He wound it around the tree, looping it over and under branches.

Louise handed a strand to Jane.

"Here, Father. Here's the next one," Jane said, holding it high.

It took five strands to wrap the entire tree, with its full, thick branches. Father plugged the final strand into the wall socket and the tree burst into color and light.

"It's beautiful!" Jane said, clapping her hands together.

"All right, girls. The rest is up to you." He put his glasses in his pocket and headed toward the kitchen for his usual cup of tea. Father always had a cup of tea in the late afternoon.

"Oh, good. We get to decorate the tree. Alice and I put out a few decorations, but she's so busy with work, we never finished." Jane opened a box of shiny red and silver balls.

"Tinsel first," Louise said, opening a package of the long silver strands. "And spread it evenly. Don't dump it on in clumps." She draped a bunch of tinsel over Jane's hand.

"Shall I get the top of the tree?" Jane asked.

"If you're careful, so you don't knock the tree over."

Jane climbed to the third step of the step stool. "I'll be careful," she said, reaching up to drape several strands over the top branches. She had to stretch to reach around the other side of the tree. She felt a little wobbly, so she straightened to get her balance. "There." She got down and went to get some more tinsel.

"Yes, that looks nice," Louise said.

Jane beamed. In past years, she'd tossed the tinsel and, according to Louise, made it messy. It was a pretty mess, though. Alice said so. But Alice wasn't as particular as Louise.

Jane and Louise had just finished putting on the shiny Christmas balls when Alice came in.

"How lovely," Alice said. "I could see the lights from the street as I drove up. Now the house looks like Christmas."

"But we have a lot more decorations to put up, don't we Louie."

"Louise," her oldest sister corrected. "Yes, Sprout, we do."

Jane giggled at the nickname Louise had given her. She knew her sister didn't like being called Louie, but she tolerated it from Jane. Jane said it to tease, but she meant it with great affection.

"Come on, Alice. Help us finish."

"I will. As soon as I put my things away."

An hour later, Louise arranged the antique papier-mâché nativity set that had come from their mother's side of the family on the fireplace mantel. The figures were beautifully detailed and were painted bright colors, from the Magi to the camels and sheep to the stable. All the figures were there except the baby Jesus in the manger. But Jane knew he wouldn't appear until one of them placed him in the manger Christmas morning. After all, that was the day they would celebrate his birth. "Can I put Jesus in the manger this year?" she asked.

Louise turned to Alice.

"Yes, that would be splendid," Alice said.

Jane clapped her hands with delight. She loved Christmas more than any other time of year. Maybe even better than her birthday. Maybe.

"And the angel said unto them, Fear not: for, behold . . ."

Louise held up her hand. "Stop there. You have the words memorized, but you need voice inflection. Like when I play a piece on the piano. Some passages are soft and others are loud. Some are fast and some are slow. I interpret the music to make it more dramatic, more intense. You need to do that with your voice. Try it again."

"And the angel said unto them, Fear not: for, behold . . ." She enunciated each word louder than the one before.

Louise shook her head. "That's not quite what I meant. Think about a song you sing in Sunday School, like 'Only A Boy Named David.' When you get to the part about the stone in the sling, you almost act it out. When you sing 'Round and round, and round, and round,' you are whirling your hand above your head like you're winding up a slingshot. Then you let go of the imaginary rock. And when you sing, 'and the giant came tumbling down,' you do motions like you're falling, and you make your voice louder. You tell the story with your voice and motions. When the angel announced Jesus' birth, it was a world-changing, life-stopping moment. For the shepherds and the wise men and everyone who heard about it, life would never be the same. So imagine how the angel announced it and see if you can convey that with your words."

"And the angel said unto them . . ." Jane stood very straight. At that point she threw her arms open wide. "Fear not: for, behold . . ."

Louise clapped. "Yes, that's much better. Pause for a moment after 'Fear not.' The sudden appearance of an angel would frighten them. They might even try to run away. Then make your joyous announcement."

Jane recited the rest of her lines. She only stumbled a couple of times. They were down to three days before the living Nativity, so she had to polish her part. "Can I go play now?"

"What are you going to do?"

"I told Carlene Moss and Fred Humbert I'd meet them at the top of our hill to go sledding." Carlene and Fred were in her class at school. They all played together a lot when they were younger, though now that they were old, sometimes Fred ignored them at school. But when he was away from his friends, he was still fun to play with. "There's just enough snow."

"All right, but only for an hour. Alice will be home by then and dinner will be ready."

"Okay."

Jane dashed out of the parlor, but heard Louise yell, "Bundle up. It's freezing outside."

As Jane put on her boots by the back door, she heard the sounds of the piano and stopped to listen. Louise was playing classical Christmas music. Jane was pretty sure it was Handel's *Messiah*. It was one of Jane's favorites, though she loved the Christmas carols too. But this was so beautiful and dramatic it made her heart ache inside. She remembered Louise playing it at church the year before. At the "Hallelujah Chorus," the choir sang along with her and everyone had stood until it was finished. Hallelujah! That's how the shepherds and wise men must have felt when they heard the angel announcing Jesus was born. That's how Jane wanted everyone to feel when she played the angel and made the announcement. As Louise said, she needed to be more dramatic. Jane wished she could fly, like an angel. That would be spectacular.

The night of the nativity was cold, but clear. Standing in the farmyard, Jane looked up and saw the Milky Way so bright that the whole sky sparkled like a million crystals. She half expected to see one of the stars turn into an angel.

She and her sisters had arrived early. There were only two other cars parked near the house. Oscar Horn and Lloyd Tynan were inside discussing the garlands that stretched across the downtown streets. Lloyd's father was the mayor and Lloyd volunteered to help with town projects. Oscar said the one in front of City Hall was coming down. Lloyd promised to fix it.

Alice and Louise got busy helping with costumes. They laid out a stack of robes.

"Oscar, Lloyd, here are your costumes," Louise said.

The men came over and put the long, loose robes that tied at the waist over their clothes. Oscar's was a plain brown. Lloyd's was bright red, with gold stripes. He was one of the three kings. Alice helped tie a white cloth on Oscar's head and wrap a red turban around Lloyd's head.

Rose and Samuel came downstairs in their costumes. As Mary and Joseph, they were dressed in simple long robes and head coverings. Caleb had on a warm, one-piece pajama set that covered his hands and feet. Caleb was going to play Jesus.

Rose laid Caleb in his cradle. "Jane, let's get you dressed in your costume. I have it here. It will fit right over your clothes."

"Okay."

"First your wings. The straps go across your chest and waist, then you slip your arms through these holes and I'll tie them in the back." Rose held up the large butterflylike wings. They were covered in a shiny gossamer white fabric and trimmed in fuzzy white fake fur.

"Wow, those are beautiful!" She slipped her arms through the holes and Rose tied the back.

"Jump up and down and see if the wings are secure," she said.

Jane spread her arms and bounced up and down and ran around the room like she was flying. The wings bobbled, but stayed in place.

"Cool! Can I have these when we're done?"

"I think we're keeping all the costumes so we can do it again next year."

"Oh. Oh well. It'll be fun to wear them tonight."

"First step into the skirt part, then hold out your arms."

Jane did as requested, and Rose pulled the robe up and slipped the full sleeves over Jane's arms, then pulled the robe to the back to fasten. Long panels of sheer material had been sewn to the top of the robe and hung down like shiny scarves to give the costume an ethereal appearance.

"We had to slit the back so it would go over the wings." Rose buttoned the back together. The costume covered her from her neck to her feet, so her sweater and the warm white tights that Louise had bought for her wouldn't show.

"Almost finished." Rose held up a white fuzzy ring about the size of a pie pan. It had two stiff wires that were attached to a smaller wire ring. "This is your halo. I have to bobby pin it to your head, so sit on a chair so I can reach."

Jane sat on a kitchen chair. Rose fastened it securely to Jane's head with half a dozen bobby pins.

"There. Now shake your head."

Jane held her head erect and didn't move. "I don't want to knock it off."

"If it's going to come off, we need to find out now, so we can fix it."

"Okay." Jane moved her head from side to side.

"Shake it harder."

Jane shook her head hard. It wobbled and felt like it was coming off, but it held.

"Good. I'll put in a couple more pins to make sure," Rose said as she stuck another bobby pin on each side. "You're ready. If you want to see your costume, go upstairs to the bathroom. There's a mirror on the back of the door.

"I will. Thanks, Rose." Jane hiked up the skirt and dashed upstairs. She went into the bathroom and shut the door, then stared, wide-eyed, at the apparition before her. The robes shimmered from the gossamer overskirt. The wings and halo were glorious. No one would doubt she was an angel tonight.

The living room and kitchen were filled with people in costumes when Jane went downstairs. There were shepherds and wise men and other people in long robes and head coverings. She hardly recognized the men in their fake brown and black and gray beards.

"Look," Samuel said. "We have a real live angel among us." He winked at Jane.

"A lovely angel," Louise said. "I wish I had a camera."

"I have one," Lloyd said. He held up a camera and told Jane to smile. She turned sideways so he could see the wings. A bright flash went off, blinding her for a few seconds.

Lloyd took several pictures of the entire group in their costumes. "I wish I could take pictures of the nativity, but I can't carry the camera and the box of gold."

"Harold Moss said he'd come out and take pictures for the next edition of the *Acorn Nutshell*," Samuel said. "And now, friends, it's time to get to our places. People will start arriving soon."

"Great," Lloyd said. "Let's go break a leg."

Jane laughed, but it was more nerves than anything. All of a sudden she had the jitters. She tried to think of her lines, but her mind was blank. She knew her costume looked great, but how would she appear if she stammered or worse? She hoped she would be able to deliver a great performance. She followed the others as everyone trooped outside and across the farmyard to the big red barn.

Jane looked up at the sky and gasped. "Look!" She pointed at a shooting star streaking across the sky over the barn. It only lasted a second, but she heard a couple of "*Oohs,*" so others saw it too. Maybe it was a sign that everything would go well. She hoped so.

Rose and Samuel had transformed the barn doorway into the city gates of Bethlehem. Jane knew the large rock wall around the doorway was made of burlap stretched over chicken wire, then painted to look like quarried stones, but she couldn't resist touching it. It felt scratchy and gave beneath her touch, but it looked real. The big door was open just wide enough to let people go inside. A few strategically placed heat lamps hanging overhead dimly lighted the barn interior.

"Young lady, you must sign in here and state your name and birth date," a man said as Jane walked in. Jane knew he was supposed to be a census taker, but a scruffy brown beard hid the gatekeeper's face, so Jane couldn't tell if she knew him.

"But I'm not a young lady. I'm an angel. See my wings?" Jane turned around so he could see her set of wings in their full splendor.

"An angel? Never seen an angel around these parts before. But everyone who comes into Bethlehem has to sign in, so the Governor can charge you taxes."

Jane giggled and signed her name.

She stepped inside the barn and was transported back two thousand years into Bethlehem on the night Jesus was born. Samuel and Rose and the people from church had transformed the old barn into a different world.

There were booths, just big enough for a person to stand behind, on both sides of the wide barn aisle. Some of the actors in the production were playing the part of the street vendors. The booth next to the census taker's was the baker's. Clarissa Cottrell and her mother were setting up their booth. They had a big basket of fresh warm buns that they'd made down at the Good Apple Bakery, one of Jane's favorite places. At least once a week she stopped at the bakery on her way home from school and bought a cookie or brownie with her allowance.

"You may have one," Clarissa said, holding out the basket.

"Thank you." Jane bit into the puffy doughnutlike bun and tasted cinnamon and walnuts and honey. So yummy. She licked her fingers as she came to the Inn, which was made from rough, unpainted boards. It didn't look like a place she would want to stay. Cyril Overstreet, the innkeeper, was standing in the doorway. She barely recognized him in the oversized robe and brown beard. He seemed an odd choice to play the part. He was a quiet, shy man, about her father's age. He played chess with her father regularly, and the two men would sit for hours, not talking, just staring at the chess pieces, then making a move once in a while. But there he was in a bathrobe instead of his usual cardigan sweater. "Move along now," he told her, but he winked. "The inn is full. No room here." Next to him, his wife, a short woman with rosy cheeks and a kind smile, offered her a small cup of hot apple cider. Jane started to take it, but she heard Louise calling her.

Jane gave Mrs. Overstreet a wistful smile. She hoped there would be cider left after the nativity. She waved at her sister and moved along, but not too quickly. Next was the stable where Mary and Joseph and Jesus would be stationed. They weren't there yet. The wooden manger, where Caleb would lie, had hay in it. There was a blanket folded up for padding. She hoped the straw wouldn't scratch him, but Rose would make sure he was all right.

Jane glanced around and saw Rose holding Caleb, who was wrapped in a blanket, talking to Alice in the next pen. Alice was in charge of the animals. She had to make sure they didn't spook or bite someone. There was the donkey, the milk cow, and several sheep. Jane looked around for the mama cat and kittens. They didn't seem to be around. Jane wished she was helping with the animals, but she supposed Alice was better suited. When Alice was a teenager, she used to bring home strays and take care of them all the time.

"Jane, you need to get up into the loft before people start arriving. They aren't supposed to see you until you appear," Louise called, beckoning her from farther down near the end of the barn, by the loft ladder.

"Coming." As she turned, she nearly tripped on her costume, then picked up the front enough to get it out of the way of her boots. She should have worn her slippers that looked like ballet shoes. Boots didn't look very angelic. She sighed and hurried over to Louise.

"I'm ready," she said.

Louise straightened Jane's robe and retied the bow at the back. After a brief examination, she nodded her head. "You look very angelic," she said. "Do you remember your lines? Do you want to go through them again?"

"I know my lines," Jane said. Louise had made her repeat them over and over since she'd arrived in Acorn Hill the week before. It was annoying because Jane didn't get to see her oldest sister very often once she had married and settled in Philadelphia. Reciting Bible verses wasn't her idea of quality sister-time.

"Good. Now you remember what you're supposed to do? When you hear the narrator say, 'There was no room for them in the inn,' you step to the edge of the loft and recite your lines. But be very careful, and hang onto that post up there," she said, pointing to a post. "We don't want you falling out of the loft."

"Don't worry. I'll be fine." She supposed Louise wasn't around enough to appreciate her abilities. She could shimmy up a tree faster and higher than any of the boys at school, and she could ride her bike with no hands. She'd climbed on the roof of their carriage house once to retrieve a ball that had gotten stuck. Going up in the barn loft was as safe as going upstairs in their home. She hiked up her robe and climbed the ladder. At the top, she looked down and grinned at her sister, who raised one eyebrow, but said nothing.

Jane had plenty of time before her part. The loft was split into two sections, one on either side of the wide aisle that stretched down the middle of the barn. She walked over to the spot above the stable where she would make her appearance and recite her lines. A single light hung above her so the people below would see her when she appeared. But it wasn't very bright. The cast had run through the whole nativity Thursday evening, and it had gone well. The shepherds and their sheep were across the barn and down toward the front in a pen, waiting for their cue. When she appeared and recited her lines, they would rise up and go down to the stable.

Jane had tried to make her lines sound exciting, but she didn't think she succeeded very well. She was perched so high above everybody, she hoped she could get their attention. Would she be loud enough for all of them to hear her? She needed a bullhorn or a whistle. But angels didn't carry whistles, as far as she knew. And angels wouldn't hang onto a post. An angel would float in the air above the crowd.

Looking around, Jane saw stacks of hay and a pitchfork. She looked up and spotted a rope hanging from the center of the barn ceiling. It looped over to a hook on the wall, where it was held by a big knot. She made her way over and examined the rope. It was thick, like a rope swing. There were two knots where someone could hold on and swing. She wondered if Samuel and Rose had used it to swing or if it had been there before they moved to the farm.

She went back to the edge of the loft and looked across to the other side. It was only about twelve feet away. The loft on the other side of the barn looked the same as the side she was standing on. There were bales of hay, but they were stacked against the back, so there was room to stand on the edge.

Suddenly, Jane had an idea. It was perfect. An angel wouldn't just stand there and hold onto a post. If the angel was truly excited, like Louise said, the angel would show it. Everyone would be so surprised.

Jane kicked off her boots, so it would look like she was in bare feet, although her feet were white from the tights. She heard a commotion, and all the players hurried to their stations.

"And it came to pass in those days, that there went out a decree from Caesar Augustus, that all the world should be taxed," a deep voice boomed out. Jane knew it was Clarissa Cottrell's father, and he was down near the barn entrance, but she couldn't see him. He was reciting the Christmas story right out of the Bible. Jane knew it well, because her father read it out loud every Christmas morning.

"And all went to be taxed, every one into his own city," he continued. "And Joseph also went up from Galilee, out of the city of Nazareth, into Judaea, unto the city of David, which is called Bethlehem, because he was of the house and lineage of David, to be taxed with Mary his espoused wife, being great with child."

Rose and Samuel walked slowly down the middle of the barn from the front door to the inn. Jane looked around to find Caleb. Louise was holding him down by the stable.

"And so it was," the announcer continued, "that, while they were there, the days were accomplished that she should be delivered. And she brought forth her firstborn son, and wrapped him in swaddling clothes, and laid him in a manger, because there was no room for them in the inn."

Mary and Joseph stopped in front of the inn and the innkeeper turned them away, but the innkeeper's wife led them to the stable.

Mary and Joseph settled in the stable and Louise carried Caleb over and handed him to Rose—er—Mary. Jane could see some of the action right beneath her as she peered down through the slats in the loft floor. She saw the manger and the top of Mary's head covering, where she sat holding the baby Jesus.

Rose placed Caleb in the manger. He was all wrapped up, so only his face was showing. Squinting, Jane could see him. He looked straight up and smiled, as if he could see her way above him. But it was dim and Rose said he still couldn't see clearly. Still, his smile seemed aimed at her. Just for her. She smiled and waved back at him.

At that moment, she realized that was her cue. The baby Jesus was laid in the manger. Without thinking, she rushed over and pulled the thick rope off the hook, grabbed the rope with each hand just above the knots, ran toward the edge and launched herself across the open divide to the other loft. As she swung over, she heard gasps of surprise. Exactly what she intended.

Jane looked down and tried to make out the faces below her, but she was moving so fast they were all a blur. She managed to let go of the rope with her upper hand and to drop onto the loft near the edge. She teetered for a moment, but got her balance. Still hanging onto the rope with one hand so she wouldn't lose it, she turned to face the startled crowd. She saw Harold Moss holding a camera, pointed at her, just as a flash went off. For a second, it blinded her. She blinked a few times, then the crowd reappeared, but she couldn't make out anyone's face. Father was there somewhere. She looked over toward the stable. Her vision cleared. She could make out Samuel and Rose staring up at her. Alice was leaning out from the animal pen, looking up, and Louise was standing next to her. Their mouths were open and their eyes wide as they all stared at her.

"And, lo, the angel of the Lord came upon them, and the glory of the Lord shone round about them, and they were sore afraid," the narrator boomed. "And the angel said unto them . . ."

Jane threw her arms open wide, still holding the rope for her return trip.

"Fear not!" She paused for dramatic effect, just as Louise had coached. "Behold, I bring you good tidings of great joy, which shall be to all people. For unto you is born this day in the city of David a Savior, which is Christ the Lord. And this shall be a sign unto you. Ye shall find the babe wrapped in swaddling clothes, lying in a manger."

The shepherds pushed their way through the crowd, leading the sheep by leashes. "Please let us through. We want to find the new baby. Did you see the angel? Have you seen the baby? Excuse us."

Jane could hear the bleating and baaing as the sheep protested.

"Can I pet him?" some child asked.

"Me too," another said. Jane knew how they felt. She loved to pet and play with the sheep, when they would let her. But she wasn't finished. She waited until the shepherds made it through the crowd and were standing right beneath her. They looked up, away from her, since she was on the wrong side of the barn. And now the stable wasn't beneath her. It was on the opposite side of the barn, under the other loft, where she was supposed to be standing. The shepherds looked around, then spotted her and turned toward her. Now she had a predicament. She had to get the crowd to turn back around so they could see the baby Jesus. First she had to finish her part.

Taking a deep breath, she shouted, "And suddenly there was with the angel a multitude of the heavenly host praising God, and saying, glory to God in the highest, and on earth peace, good will toward men."

Everyone was watching her. She reached up and grabbed the rope above the knots, as before.

"Jane, no!" Louise yelled, but it was too late. She kicked off, sailing back toward the other side. But as she swung her legs forward, her feet caught in the hem of her dress. If she let go, she wouldn't be able to land on her feet, and might not even make it into the loft. Jane held on, and the rope swung back away from the other side of the loft, and she swung gently, suspended above the crowd.

Ahs of alarm rose from beneath her. Her feet were at least a yard above the heads of the tallest people in the crowd.

"Hang on, Jane. We'll get you down," some man shouted.

"I'll get a ladder," another voice said, and he moved toward the door. She didn't know who it was, but she couldn't hang there. The nativity play wasn't finished. She had to get out of the way, so the play could continue. Besides, she could do this. She'd swung on rope swings before. No problem. So she kicked out with her feet and got to swinging. It took several kicks and swings to get close enough to the loft in back of her to push off. She swung across, then back, then across, gaining momentum.

"Jane, stop. We'll get you down," someone called out. A woman. Maybe it was Mrs. Overstreet. But she couldn't stop. She was nearly there. Each time she swung, she heard murmurs and words of alarm. She knew she wouldn't drop, but they didn't know how good she was at swinging from trees. A couple more swings, and she could get over to the other loft and out of sight. Then they would be facing the stable.

"Jane, let go. I'll catch you," a deep male voice said.

Jane recognized her father's voice. Oh no! She would knock him flat if she let go. Her feet were free of the robe now. She swung backward at full speed and bent her knees, ready to connect with the loft edge. When it was just beneath her, she kicked off as hard as she could and sailed toward the other loft.

As she got close, she realized it was higher than the other side. Or the rope was longer. She didn't know what was wrong, but it was above her feet. She swung her feet forward to get on top of it and missed, crashing into the edge with her shin. Her body propelled forward. She reached out and grabbed the upright support and her upper body flopped over the edge. She scrambled to grasp hold on the loft and got her fingers around the edge of a floor plank. Letting go of the rope with her other hand, she grabbed the floor and clung to it, stunned. The breath was knocked out of her, and her legs dangled over the side.

Caleb let out a cry. She must have startled him, poor baby. He stopped for a second, long enough to take in a deep breath, then he began to wail. Jane felt like crying along with him. But at least he had announced his presence and everyone could turn their attention back to him.

Jane had experience getting out of embarrassing situations. She knew she had to move quickly. She wiggled her body and inched up onto the loft. There were gasps beneath her. She heard a rip. Felt sharp pain in her leg. No time to think about that. She scrambled up and out of sight, then lay on the hay-strewn plank floor, trying to catch her breath.

"Jane?" came a voice from below.

"I'm okay," she said, not at all certain it was the truth, but the show must go on. "Please forget about me."

There were a few moments of silence, then her father said, "Let's continue."

"And it came to pass," the booming voice of the narrator said, "when the angels were gone away from them into heaven, the shepherds hastened to Bethlehem and found Mary, and Joseph, and the babe lying in a manger."

Saved. Jane rolled over on her back and tried to sit up. It hurt. Everything hurt. Especially her leg. She looked down. Even in the dim light, she could see a long rip in her white tights and blood all over her leg. It stung and ached like the dickens. And she was mortified. She'd ruined the nativity. She'd let down Rose and Samuel and Louise and Alice and Father. She'd wanted so badly to be the best angel ever, but she'd failed. Her wings were all bent up. Her halo was hanging askew. The beautiful gossamer costume was ripped and bloody. Jane pulled herself across the hay to a corner behind a stack of hay bales, where no one could see her.

Curling up in a ball, Jane covered her face with her hands. She could feel the wetness of the tears streaking down her cheeks. Burying her face in her arms, she wept as the nativity continued beneath her. She heard the three kings arriving, asking the way to see the newborn king.

"Jane, where are you, sweetheart?"

It was Father. She didn't want him to see her, but oh, how she wanted to cry on his strong shoulder. She heard him making his way across the loft. Then he was bending over her.

"There you are. Oh, Jane." She heard his sigh, but wasn't sure if it was resignation at his wayward daughter or relief that she was all right. He dropped down onto his knees beside her.

"Are you all right? Let me see your leg. I know you hit it hard."

Jane rolled halfway over and tried to stretch out her leg so he could see. He wiped her tears with his handkerchief. Then he looked at her leg.

"It's hard to tell if you broke it, but you have a nasty cut," he said. He dabbed at it with his handkerchief.

Jane flinched. It hurt so bad.

"It has stopped bleeding, but it will probably start again when we move you. I need to get you down and out of here and take you to the doctor."

"No, Father, please. I don't want to mess up the nativity any more. I'll stay here until it's finished. I'll be all right." She tried to smile. She brushed away tears with the back of her hand.

He looked into her face for a moment, then sat down in the hay, his back against the bales. "I'll stay with you." He gently gathered her in his arms, careful not to hurt her leg.

He was wearing his second-best white shirt and his best wool sweater. Jane was conscious that she was about to ruin his clothes, too, but he held her close, and she couldn't resist. She curled up against him and let her tears flow, choking back sobs so no one else could hear her.

"I'm s-sorry. I ruined everything again. I d-didn't mean to."

"Sweetheart, you were the most amazing angel I've ever seen." She looked up at his face, trying to see if he was serious. "Really?"

He smoothed her hair back away from her face. It was sticking to her tears. "Truly. And the nativity is almost over. Then we'll get you out of here."

"Okay." Jane closed her eyes. The leg was throbbing hard now. She pressed her lips together and tried to listen to the rest of the nativity.

She must have dozed off. Next thing she knew, Alice was bending over her leg. She pressed her fingers against the bone and Jane cried out. She couldn't help it.

"Sorry," Alice said. "I've got to see if it's broken."

She felt up and down the bone just above and below the cut, then pressed right against it with their father's handkerchief. Jane bit her lip so she wouldn't scream.

"I don't think it's broken. We can't do stitches on the shin. The skin is too tight. I can make butterfly bandages. I have my nursing bag in the car. I'll go get it and we'll clean you up."

"Let's get her down from the loft first," Father said.

"I think we should get it bandaged first," Alice said. "Moving her first will start the bleeding again."

"All right. We'll wait here."

Alice went back to the ladder and descended. Jane could hear her talking to the others.

"Is she all right?" Jane recognized Rose's voice.

"She has a nasty scrape on her shin, but otherwise, I think she's all right."

"I told you she would figure out a way to ruin the nativity," Jane heard, and couldn't mistake the voice of Florence Simpson. As much as she hated it, Mrs. Simpson was right. She had ruined it.

"That's not true," Samuel's voice said. "Jane was a fine angel. No one will ever forget her announcement." Jane heard him laugh.

"I suspect it was my fault," Louise said. "I coached her and told her to create an emotional experience for the audience."

"She certainly did that," Rose said. "I think she's a natural actress."

"She's a natural hoyden," Florence said.

"Florence, let's get out of here and let these people take care of what they need to do," Ronald Simpson said.

"I just wanted to help," she objected.

"Yes, dear." Their voices were fading. Jane was glad. She felt embarrassed enough without having to face Mrs. Simpson. She didn't want to ever face her again.

"I've got to get my medical bag," Jane heard Alice say.

"How can I help?" Louise asked.

"I need some clean, damp cloths."

"We'll use clean burp cloths. I have plenty of them," Rose said. I'll come with you and take Caleb inside. He's so tired."

"He was a wonderful baby Jesus," Louise said.

"He was, wasn't he? And while you get Jane fixed up and bring her down from that loft, I'll make some tea and cocoa. Bring her in the house and she can rest while you all get ready to leave."

"I'll rig a sling," Samuel said. "That'll be the best way to get her down without hurting her."

Alice returned in a few moments and climbed up to the loft. She spread a clean receiving blanket beneath Jane's leg, then cut away the torn white tights.

"This is going to sting, I'm afraid, but I've got to clean it up. Hold still." She wiped the leg with a damp cloth, then dabbed and wiped the wound with cotton soaked in alcohol.

"*Ouch*. That hurts," Jane cried, trying to keep from jerking her leg away.

Alice looked more closely. "It's hard to see in this light, but I think you're full of splinters. I can't get them out now, though. I'll have to do that at home. For now, I'm going to bind this up."

Alice smeared antibiotic ointment on the cut, then covered it with gauze. She cut butterfly bandages out of tape and stretched six of them across Jane's shin, pulling the skin together. Then she wrapped Jane's lower leg with an Ace bandage.

"There. That should hold it for now."

Samuel appeared up the ladder with a canvas sling and rope. Jane had seen it before. Samuel used it to hold the sheep when he weighed them.

"Lloyd and Cyril are down below ready to help. We'll lower Jane in the sling."

Samuel spread the sling on the ground, then Father carefully set Jane in it.

"We're going to tie you in, so you can't fall out," Samuel said. He threaded rope through rings in the edge of the canvas and pulled it taut, then knotted it.

"Ready?"

Jane nodded.

"Rev. Howard, if you'll take that end of the rope and wrap it around the post once, so you can control it, I'll take this side and we'll lower her down. Just take it slow. We need to be careful not to bump her leg. And Jane, hold on, and no swinging."

"I won't. I promise."

"Good. Ready?"

"Ready," Father responded.

As the sling slowly lowered, Jane could hear two men talking in the stall where Alice had been with the animals.

"Good thing you saw that lamp hit the hay," one said. "How did it happen?"

"The angel kicked it with her foot when she landed against the loft. It was hanging from a wire hook. It came off and went sailing into a pile of hay. I had my eye on those lamps, since we had so many people in here. I was afraid some kid would bump one, and I'm supersensitive to those lamps since that fire over at the Walden place last week. Burned the barn to the ground. It started from a heat lamp. They run hot and that hay is dry."

"Well, it was a kid. Jane. I heard about the Walden place. Bad luck. Gotta be so careful."

"Yeah. Their barn wasn't full of people, though, and that hay was already hot when I got to it."

"*Phew.* Then I guess you just saved some lives."

"Naw. It wasn't anything."

"Not true. If I haven't told you before, it's great to have you back."

"Thanks, Mr. Horn."

"Call me Oscar."

When she was nearly down, Jane looked over to see Oscar Horn talking to Derek Grollier, who had just returned from the war in Vietnam. From the sounds of their conversation, she nearly had burned the barn down. That was worse than any bump on her leg. Jane felt terrible. All their friends. Baby Caleb and Rose and Samuel and all the people from town and her own family and all the animals. The thought of what could have happened crushed her. Did Samuel and Rose know? Had Samuel and Father overheard? Had Lloyd and Cyril heard the men talking? If not yet, surely they would all find out. She needed to make amends, but she didn't know what to do.

After they set Jane in an overstuffed chair with a footstool to prop up her injured leg, the men went back to the barn to finish their work. Alice took another look at her leg, which had started bleeding again, and Louise helped Rose in the kitchen. Rose brought an ice bag, which Alice placed over the wound on Jane's shin. Louise brought a cup of hot cocoa for Jane, but she couldn't drink it. She couldn't get it past the lump in her throat.

She started to cry.

"Does your leg hurt?" Alice asked.

Jane sniffled and shook her head. "I ruined the angel costume you made," she said. "It was so beautiful."

"Don't be upset about the costume. We can always make another one. I'm more concerned about your leg. I think you'll be all right tonight. You could have a hairline fracture, but it doesn't appear to be broken. I'll take you to the hospital tomorrow so you can get an X-ray and have a doctor look at it."

"I'm all right, Alice. It's just a bruise. You don't need to take me to the hospital. It'll be fine by tomorrow." Jane didn't know if that was true, but she was determined not to cause any more trouble. Why had she thought she had to fly across the barn?

Rose went upstairs to put Caleb to bed. Father came in. Lloyd and the others had left. Samuel was still in the barn, finishing nightly chores.

"Let's get you home, Jane. I'll carry you to the car," her father said.

"I can walk, Father."

"Perhaps you can, but this time, I will carry you."

Though he spoke with a gentle voice, Jane didn't argue.

Alice helped her put on her coat. Then her father lifted her into his arms. He was tall and strong, but Jane felt silly. She was twelve—too big to be carried. She put her arms around his neck and leaned her head against his shoulder. She was so tired and her leg had begun to throb again. She needed to talk to him and to Rose and Samuel and apologize, but it would have to wait. She didn't want to delay too long, or she would lose her courage to face them. Perhaps tomorrow.

The next morning, explaining to the doctor how she had injured her leg embarrassed Jane all over again. It had seemed like such a good idea at the time. Swinging from that rope up into the loft should have been easy. She had swung from trees, branch to branch, before. She still needed to apologize to Samuel and Rose and Father, and that thought made her stomach ache.

"You are fortunate," the doctor said after he'd seen the X-ray. "The bone is bruised, but not broken. Your sister has taken good care of you, getting the wound clean and bandaged. I want you to keep the leg raised and keep ice on it for a couple of days, and stay off of it. When you have to move around, use the crutches until the swelling goes down. Walking on it will hurt for a couple of weeks, but you can resume normal activity."

The doctor wrapped Jane's lower leg, from the ankle up to her knee, with an elasticized bandage. "This will help the blood flow away from the injured site." He looked at Alice. "Rewrap this every day as needed."

Alice nodded. Jane knew with Alice taking care of her and Louise at the house, she would not be able to get out and play. She would have preferred a cast. At least then she could collect signatures and draw pictures on it. A bruise wasn't as exciting as a broken leg. Jane knew she was in for a boring time. At least she had one more Nancy Drew book from the library to read. She would have to read slowly.

Jane was sitting in the parlor in an easy chair, her leg propped up on an ottoman and pillows. She loved hearing the fire crackle and pop and the flames dance in the fireplace, but sitting still was harder than she'd expected. She felt like an invalid, and wasn't happy about it. She supposed her confinement was just penance for ruining the living Nativity and nearly burning down the Bellwoods' barn. Guilt was gnawing at her stomach.

Louise had brought a tray with tomato soup and crackers for lunch. She'd tucked a towel under Jane's chin as a bib. She ate, though she wasn't hungry. She had finished and the tray was still on her lap. She wanted to get up and take it back to the kitchen so she could read her book, but she wasn't supposed to get up, and she didn't want to upset her sisters or bring attention to herself. She had caused enough trouble.

Jane heard voices coming from the kitchen. Friends usually parked in back of the house and used the back door.

Louise appeared in the doorway. "Jane, look who's come to see you? Oh, let me get that tray out of here." She swooped in and lifted the tray and towel. Rose and Samuel Bellwood were right behind her. Samuel was carrying a portable bassinet with a handle. He'd made it out of wood, and Rose had lined it with a pad and quilts. Caleb was sound asleep in it. Samuel set it down between two chairs.

"Have a seat," Louise said. "I'll put this in the kitchen and make tea."

Jane heard Louise announce their visitors to their father, who was in his study.

"How are you feeling, Jane?" Rose asked. "We heard the good news that your leg isn't broken. But I'm sure it hurts."

"It's not too bad," Jane said, blushing.

Samuel stood when her father entered the room.

"Good afternoon," Father said. "How nice of you to stop by to cheer up our Jane. It's rather quiet around here. Not much entertainment for an invalid."

"I don't need to be entertained, Father. But I'm happy to see you," she said, turning to address their guests. In truth, she had dreaded facing them. Now she must. Especially with Father there.

"I brought some custard for you," Rose said. "It's rich, with fresh cream and eggs. My mother always made it whenever one of us kids was hurt or sick. I believe it helped us heal faster. In any case, it's a treat. I made enough so you could all have some."

"Thank you," Jane said. "I love custard." Jane smiled to cover up her distress and hoped no one would notice. She didn't deserve Rose's kindness.

Alice and Louise came in carrying the teapot and a tray with cream and sugar and Linzer cookies that Louise had made for Christmas.

Louise gave Jane an odd look when she passed up a cookie and a cup of tea. When everyone was served, Jane cleared her throat.

"I am sorry," she said, hanging her head and almost hoping no one would hear her.

"What did you say, Jane?" her father asked.

She looked up. They were all staring at her. She cleared her throat again. "I—I . . ." She took a deep breath. "I'm sorry that I ruined the living Nativity and almost burned down the barn. I wanted to make the angel's part *rememberable*."

Rose shook her head side to side, but didn't speak. Samuel leaned forward, his elbows on his knees, his large hands fisted against his chin. He didn't frown or smile—just listened. Alice had on her nurse look—concerned and nodding with sympathy. Jane knew that look well. And Louise sat back and listened with one eyebrow raised. No frown. No smile. Nothing to indicate what she was thinking. Jane looked at her father. His head was bent slightly to one side. He was watching her and listening. His expression gave away nothing, but his eyes held kindness, and that was her undoing. A tear leaked out the side of her eye. She rubbed it away with the back of her hand.

"I shouldn't have swung on the rope. But I knew I could do it. I've swung on lots of ropes before. I won't do it again."

"Jane, you didn't ruin the nativity," Rose said, reaching her hand out toward Jane. "You made the announcement with clarity and a great deal of enthusiasm. Then you got everyone's attention turned onto the stable, and you disappeared from view. That was the angel's role, and you did it well. Although the flying through the air part was unexpected, it was what an angel would do. I admit I was concerned about you. Your leg hit that beam hard. I could hear it."

"Apology accepted," Samuel said. "But you don't need to promise not to swing on ropes again. Although please don't try it without having someone examine the rope."

"Thank you. I won't," Jane said. "But I heard that I knocked down a lamp and almost started a fire. If Derek Grollier hadn't seen it fall. . ." Jane shuddered, thinking what could have happened.

"That was my fault for hanging the lamp so close to the where someone could bump into it. I know better. And I talked to Derek. Thanked him. He'd been looking for work since he got out of the army and came home. I guess word got around about his quick thinking at the barn. This morning the fire chief offered him a job with the fire department and they're going to train him. He said it was odd the way things worked out. He'd been applying for jobs and praying for something to open. He's very excited about getting the job."

Jane exhaled. "That's good. I'm glad. He's real nice and treats me like I'm his age, although I know he's a lot older than me."

"Yeah, like almost my age," Alice said.

"And mine," Rose said, smiling.

Their smiles lifted some of her guilt, but she glanced at Samuel, and he wasn't smiling.

"Jane, I went into the loft this morning. I hadn't paid attention to that rope before. It was dark in there last night, so you wouldn't have seen, but today the light was streaming in through the cracks in the walls. Where it looped over the roof beam, the rope was rubbing against a big spike. I gave it a little tug and the whole rope came crashing down. Why it didn't break under your weight last night . . ." He shook his head as if in disbelief. "I don't know. The slightest weight should have snapped it. Doesn't make any sense to me. You could have been—probably should have been seriously hurt. But I thank the Lord you weren't."

Rose's smile vanished. Her face paled. "Samuel, you didn't tell me."

"I knew you'd be upset," he said. "But Jane needs to know how dangerous ropes and barns can be. I'd have had a hard time forgiving myself if something had happened to you."

Or someday to little Caleb, Jane thought with horror. If she hadn't swung on it, Samuel might not have noticed it until it was too late. She had felt completely secure on the rope, until she couldn't swing hard enough to reach the loft. She had wiggled and tugged, never considering the rope might be old and frayed. She looked to see her father's reaction.

All the color had drained from Father's face. He closed his eyes a moment and sighed. Then he looked at her.

"My dear, impetuous Jane. You have such enthusiasm for life, I have wondered more than once how your guardian angels can keep up with you. Perhaps you weren't the only angel in the loft last night. The Bible says in Psalms 91:11-12, 'For He shall give His angels charge over thee, to keep thee in all thy ways. They shall bear thee up in their hands, lest thou dash thy foot against a stone.'

"Father, do you really think an angel protected me?" Jane considered it for a moment. She remembered how bright the stars were the night before, making her think of angels. She remembered the shooting star that streaked straight at the barn.

"I don't know, Jane. I can only tell you what the Bible says, and what I see. This isn't the first time you have avoided dire consequences. Last night you were saved from serious injury, and the barn was protected. Someone must have been watching out for us all." He shook his head. "Do take pity on those poor angels, though."

"At least they get a few days to rest while you are off your feet," Louise said.

"I love the thought of angels visiting our barn and protecting us all," Rose said. "When I think what could have happened . . ." She shuddered, then looked at Jane and smiled. "But it didn't. I am very thankful for such a wonderful night for our living Nativity. I heard lots of people enjoyed it. And I am going to believe that our living Nativity had a real-live miracle."

Jane looked around, wondering if an angel was watching now. Father was right. From now on she would be more careful. Angels were mighty powerful, but she didn't have to make them work so hard.

$\mathcal{P}$erhaps in retrospect, that night was a bit eventful," Jane said. "I'm sorry if I gave you gray hair, Louie. I didn't mean to."

"You gave Mother her gray hair? I thought I did."

The sisters turned to see Cynthia enter the living room. She was dressed in herringbone wool slacks and a teal-green cashmere sweater. Her dark hair was sleek and smooth and her blue eyes shiny with the anticipation of the holiday. Jane jumped up and gave her a hug. "Happy Christmas! Come sit with us and I'll get you some coffee. We were just reminiscing. And I only gave your mother her *first* gray hair. You must have given her the rest."

Cynthia laughed and hugged Jane back, then hugged Alice and went to sit next to Louise. "Merry Christmas, Mother. Did I give you your gray hair? It makes you look so sophisticated and regal, I'm glad I could contribute."

"Silly girl." Louise kissed her daughter's cheek.

"I suppose I caused you concern too, Alice," Jane said. "Although you are always so composed in an emergency. You're a perfect nurse."

"I got plenty of practice on you," Alice said, her eyes sparkling with humor. "You did outgrow your hijinks, though not your lively spirits, thank the Lord. I believe you keep us all young."

"Well, that's a good thing. Right?"

"You also proved Florence wrong," Louise said. "You grew up just fine. Better than fine. And that craft party at her house might have been the beginning of your artistic endeavors. The ornament you made for me is one of my favorites. It's hanging right up there near the top of the tree." She pointed to the sparkly silver cone, still intact. "I couldn't believe you made it when you were only twelve."

"Clarissa helped me with that and many other projects as I grew up. And you gave me my first real art set."

"You're a fabulous artist, Aunt Jane."

"Thank you, dear. We've each been blessed with a special talent."

"*Yoo-hoo!*" Aunt Ethel came sailing in from the kitchen. She was carrying two shiny bags with large bows of curly ribbon in each hand. With her bright red Christmas sweater, adorned with beaded poinsettias, her titian-red hair artfully coiffed, and her cheeks rosy red from the cold morning, she was the perfect picture of Christmas cheer. "Here you are. Merry Christmas, my dear nieces. I hope I'm not late for breakfast." She set the bags under the tree.

"You're just in time, Auntie. I need to take the strata out of the oven and I'll be ready to serve." Jane gave her aunt a hug, then left the room.

"I'll help Jane serve. You all can go to the dining room," Alice said. She followed Jane out.

"You were telling stories when I came down," Cynthia said. "I hope I didn't miss anything."

"You were so tired last night, we decided to let you sleep in," Louise said. "We read the Christmas story out of the Bible and that set off some reminiscing."

"I wish I'd been down to hear it. I always love hearing the real Christmas story. It just makes the day more meaningful."

"I'm sorry I missed it too. I remember Daniel reading it every year. I do miss him so," Ethel said. She was Rev. Howard's half-sister, born when he was in his late teens. Ethel and her husband Bob had lived on a farm outside of town. After Jane was born and the girls' mother died, she had helped Daniel with the girls—especially Jane.

"Come on, Auntie. Let's not miss breakfast." Cynthia put her arm around her great-aunt and ushered her to the dining room.

Louise sighed with contentment. As she rose, she looked at the stockings hung from the mantel. Each stocking was home-made. Their mother had sewed each one with loving detail for her daughters. Even Jane's had been made in anticipation of her birth. Since Madeleine had died soon after giving birth, Aunt Ethel had added Jane's name to her stocking. They still looked lovely, except for Cynthia's. It looked a little wonky. It was old and made from inexpensive quilted fabric and the pattern had faded over the years. The C and the Y in her name were crooked. Louise tried to straighten the letters. The hand stitching looked like a child had done it, and the rickrack around the top was coming unglued.

"Louise!" Jane called. "Come eat!"

"I'm coming." She left the living room and hurried to the dining room, where everyone was seated, waiting for her.

The table was laden with foods that evoked strong memories. Jane had discovered their mother's cookbook and had revived favorite recipes from when Louise was a child. Jane added her own touches to the Christmas Strata, giving it endless variety. She hadn't changed the Monkey Bread, though. As the oldest, Louise remembered their mother preparing the gooey, sweet bread and allowing her to help. Now she was happy to leave the cooking to Jane, who'd never had the chance to cook with their mother.

"Sorry," she said as she sat down.

"Last one gets to say grace," Jane said, grinning.

"I'd be delighted," Louise said. They all bowed their heads. "Lord, we thank you for this special day when we celebrate your birth. Thank you for our loving family and the joy we have together. Thank you for this meal and for the sweet memories it brings of loved ones who are now with you. We ask your blessing on the food and on our time together. In Jesus' name. Amen.

"Everything looks and smells delicious." Louise took a serving of the egg strata. "What is in the strata this year, Jane?"

"It's pretty basic. I used ham and cheese, but I tweaked it a bit to make it taste like a Monte Cristo sandwich. You can sprinkle a dash of powdered sugar on it, or some maple syrup."

"I'll try it with the sugar." She passed the dish to Alice. As she placed a cloth napkin in her lap, she said, "I was late because I was trying to straighten Cynthia's stocking. I'm afraid it's seen better days. I'm thinking I need to make a new one, or buy a handmade one. I've seen some lovely personalized Christmas stockings."

"Oh no. I love it the way it is," Cynthia said. "I can't imagine Christmas with a different stocking."

"But darling, it's as old as you are."

"Really? I didn't realize that. Where did it come from?"

"Have I not told you that story?" Louise said. "Well . . ."

Louise's Christmas Memory

*H*ow can such a tiny girl make so much noise?" Louise murmured as she cradled her crying baby on her shoulder.

Carrying Cynthia to the window that overlooked the street in front of their Philadelphia apartment, she wondered if her first-born was destined to be an opera singer. She certainly had the lungs for it. Louise hoped she'd inherited her parents' love of music, but only time would tell if their talent had been passed on to her.

"Hush, baby, hush," Louise cooed, praying her three-month-old infant would find relief from her colic.

Gently falling snow was blanketing the neighborhood of aging brownstones, giving it a charm it lacked in the harsh light of day. The soft yellow glow from the old-fashioned street lights reminded Louise of a Christmas card scene, and indeed it was less than two weeks until the celebration of Christ's birth.

"Daddy should be home soon," she told her baby.

Even when Cynthia was red-faced and tear-streaked, she was the most beautiful human being Louise had ever seen. Her perfectly formed miniature toes and fingers were marvels to behold, and the pale blonde hair on her head was unimaginably soft against her mother's cheek. She even had her own special scent, sweeter than talc and more beguiling than the finest perfume.

Movement seemed to calm her baby, so Louise paced the small apartment, and looked at the ingredients she'd optimistically laid out for Christmas cookies. She so wanted to follow the Christmas traditions her mother started when Louise was a baby. Although Cynthia was too young to know or remember, it was still her first Christmas. Everything had to be perfect.

Louise looked out the window again. When would Eliot get home? She knew he was busy with end-of-semester activities at the conservatory, but his homecoming was the highlight of her day. She loved him even more now that they'd become parents together. He didn't have movie-star good looks, and lately he seemed a little too thin, but to her he was the handsomest man alive.

Cynthia gradually stopped crying, and Louise peeked at her little face nestled in a soft pink flannel blanket embroidered with teddy bears. It was one of three hand-stitched by her aunt Alice. Her tiny eyes were closed, and Louise carefully laid her in the wooden cradle Louise's father had repainted for her. It had been in the attic at his home since her youngest sister Jane had outgrown it. She gently pulled a warm fleece blanket over her baby and stepped away.

Her quiet stealth didn't work. Before she could get the flour for her cookies measured, Cynthia protested loudly. She was wide awake and clenching her little fists.

"Oh, sweetheart," Louise said picking her up again. "It's too soon to eat again. Don't you know little girls need sleep?"

Louise smiled in spite of her weariness. Although she'd read Dr. Spock's book about raising children, nothing she remembered made her less concerned or less tired. She'd already called the pediatrician twice since bringing Cynthia home from the hospital, but he didn't seem worried about her baby's tummy troubles. 'She'll outgrow it' did nothing to reassure a new mother with a colicky baby.

The early darkness of December made it feel even more like bedtime, but Cynthia was having none of it. Louise sat and rocked her in the wooden chair that had been their first furniture purchase after she became pregnant. It didn't do much good to soothe the baby, but Louise was glad to get off her feet for a bit. She felt herself drifting toward sleep, and she fought it, afraid of dropping her baby if she dozed off.

The sound of Eliot coming in the door couldn't have been more welcome.

"How are my girls?" he asked, walking into the living room, his hair damp from melting snowflakes.

"One of us is exhausted," Louise said, rising to receive his light kiss. "Unfortunately, it's not Cynthia. She seems determined to stay up all night."

"Every time I see her, I can't quite believe she's ours to keep," her husband said, looking at the baby with adoring eyes. "I feel so blessed to have you and Cynthia in my life."

"I'm afraid you won't appreciate your wife quite so much after I warm up yesterday's tuna casserole for dinner," Louise teased.

"You know I eat to live, not live to eat," he said repeating what he always said when dinner was unappetizing. Unfortunately, that was more frequent these days, as Louise struggled to be both wife and mother.

She hurried to the kitchenette, the area that passed for a kitchen in the small apartment. Somehow, she managed to put the leftover casserole in the oven while holding the baby. Maybe she could start making her mother's cookie recipe as it heated.

When Eliot had washed up and changed into an old sweatshirt he'd found in the basket of clean but unfolded laundry, he came into the kitchen and took his daughter.

"Let me hold her," he said. "It's the highlight of my day."

"Did you have a bad day?" Louise asked, trying to sound like a supportive wife, even though she was reeling from fatigue.

"No, things went smoothly." He looked at the cookie cutters scattered on the counter. "You're not going to bake tonight, are you?"

"I have to," Louise said. "It wouldn't be Christmas without homemade cookies. And remember, I have to make extra for your departmental party."

"Store-bought cookies would be fine for that. I hate to see you slaving away in kitchen when you're so tired." He rocked Cynthia in his arms, and she cooed happily for him.

"I love making traditional Christmas cookies." She held up angel, tree, and bell-shaped tin cookie cutters with little red and green wooden handles. "It wouldn't seem right if I didn't make Mother's special recipe. She always made a thin white icing out of powdered sugar. When I was old enough, I always got to sprinkle red and green colored sugar on them."

"Still, you don't need to make them for my school party. Other people will be bringing things too."

"Eliot Smith, I won't have you taking those neon-colored Christmas cookies I've seen in the grocery store. Anyway, it is less expensive to make them myself. I already have the ingredients."

"I just hate to see you working so hard."

"It's not work. I love carrying on the traditions my mother started. She had so many, and I want to do that for Cynthia. I loved how every year she gave Alice and me an ornament as a keepsake. I still have all of mine."

"Yes, you put them on our little tree last year," he said. "It was nice to hear you tell about the significance of each one."

"And I still have the stocking she made for me when I was a baby. She made one for each of us, Jane also, though she didn't get to finish that one." Louise sighed deeply. Her mother had died giving birth to Jane, so Jane never got to know their mother. "Aunt Ethel later finished it by embroidering Jane's name on it. I want to carry on that tradition for Cynthia too."

"That's a lovely tradition. Next year you'll have to make one for Cynthia," he said, cooing at his tiny daughter as he sat at the Formica and chrome table for dinner.

"No, I'm going to make Cynthia's this Christmas. It's a family tradition, and I can't wait to get the material and start it. After all, I have Mother's old sewing machine, so there's no reason not to."

"That machine is older than I am," Eliot said.

"I doubt that!" His age was a running joke between them, but most of the time Louise forgot he was fifteen years older than she was. In fact, he enjoyed clowning around so much, Louise sometimes felt like the older one.

When the casserole was hot enough, she took a head of lettuce from the refrigerator and chopped off a wedge for both of them, dribbling French dressing over each serving. It wasn't much of a vegetable, but it was green—sort of. Eliot never complained about her less-than-expert meal preparations, but lately she'd been wishing she had time to do better for him.

By the time dinner was ready, Cynthia had dropped off to sleep in her father's arms, and he had better luck laying her down. She settled into a sound sleep, one that would last hours instead of minutes, Louise hoped.

She brought out a bowl of strawberry gelatin, but Eliot declined. He didn't have a sweet tooth, and even if he had, the somewhat rubbery red dessert didn't look that appealing. She'd tried to save money by buying an unknown brand, but it wasn't very tasty.

In fact, she'd been unusually frugal the past month, and had managed to save up enough to buy some really nice fabric for Cynthia's Christmas stocking. She felt a bit guilty about scrimping on groceries, but Eliot wasn't one to notice or complain.

After they'd finished eating, they sat at the table sharing the day's events. A strident ring from their old black phone interrupted their conversation.

"I guess I have to get it," Louise said, enjoying the quiet minutes with her husband too much to move. Maybe she would wait until morning to mix up the cookies.

"Louise, this is Reverend Baker," a familiar voice said. "I hope I'm not interrupting your supper."

"No, not at all, we've finished."

"How is that new bundle of joy?"

It seemed a bit unusual for the minister of their church to call, but she soon learned the reason.

"We've had something of a crisis," he explained. "Mrs. Taylor had a nasty fall on the ice and broke her right arm."

Louise's heart sank. She knew exactly what that meant. The choir director wouldn't be able to lead the Christmas concert. She'd been asked to substitute once before when Mrs. Taylor had been ill.

"I know how busy you must be with a new baby," the minister continued, "but is there any possibility you could fill in for her? You did such a fine job the last time."

How could she turn down such an important request? Part of her very much wanted to grab the opportunity, but how would she fit it into the crowded days before Christmas? She gave Eliot a panicky look, but there was no way she could say no. Her father was a minister, and she knew how hard it could be to serve as spiritual counselor and the head of a church.

"Yes, I can," Louise said a bit bleakly.

Rev. Baker didn't seem to hear her reluctance. He thanked her profusely and told her the rehearsal times.

"Thank you so much, Louise. The congregation would be terribly disappointed if we had to cancel the Christmas program."

Eliot looked unhappy when she hung up.

"You just took on another job," he said with a worried frown.

"The choir director fell on ice and broke her arm."

"Darling, don't tell me you agreed to direct the Christmas concert?"

"I did. I'm sorry it will make more work for you when you're so busy with end-of-semester duties."

"You're the one who's overworked already. Maybe you can put off making a stocking for Cynthia until next Christmas. She won't know the difference."

"But I will," Louise insisted stubbornly.

"At least cut back on making cookies," Eliot suggested mildly.

Before Louise could argue against that idea, Cynthia cried out for attention.

"It's time to feed her," her mother said.

No matter how much she had to do before Christmas, Louise was determined to carry out all the wonderful traditions her mother had started. She silently thanked the Lord for an understanding husband, the opportunity to serve her church, and beautiful memories of her beloved mother.

When Cynthia cried at five in the morning the next day, Louise felt as though she hadn't slept at all. The baby's 2:00 AM feeding hadn't gone well, and it had taken a while to get her back to sleep.

"Coming, my little darling," Louise said in a soft voice, hurrying to pick her up before she woke Eliot. He needed to sleep until the alarm rang.

By the time Cynthia was fed, changed, and rocked back to sleep, Louise felt too wide awake to bother going back to bed. In fact, this was the perfect time to mix up her Christmas cookies before she fixed breakfast for her husband.

Besides making cookies, she looked forward to buying material for Cynthia's Christmas stocking today. She'd already checked nearby stores without finding the red quilted material she'd set her heart on. This afternoon her neighbor Maxine was going to baby-sit long enough for Louise to take a bus to the city center, where the venerable department store, Wanamaker's, was located. It was the oldest business of its type in Philadelphia, and one of the first in the country. She had high hopes of finding some spectacular material in their yard goods department.

She hoped she could catch a direct bus without too much waiting, especially on the homeward trip. Her first concert rehearsal was tonight, and she still had to go over the music. Fortunately, Rev. Baker was dropping it off at their apartment this afternoon, which saved her a trip to the church.

For nearly an hour, she lost herself in the pleasure of baking. It wasn't something she did often or particularly well, but rolling dough and cutting out the cookies brought back joyful memories of helping her mother. Now she had to time the baking so the cookies didn't get too brown. The vintage gas stove that came with the apartment left a lot to be desired, so she'd have to check the oven frequently to be sure nothing burned. She couldn't afford to waste time or ingredients, especially when she wanted nice cookies for Eliot's party.

"What are you doing?" her husband asked in a groggy voice, coming into the kitchen.

"I didn't hear the alarm," she said. She didn't answer his question because she obviously was making cookies.

"I woke up a few minutes early and turned it off."

He sat down at the table in his tattered woolen robe, one he'd had long before they met. Louise wished she could afford to get him a new one for Christmas, maybe something spiffy with velvet lapels, but it was out of the question this year. They were putting aside a part of his salary every payday, hoping to save enough for a down payment on a house. They were already outgrowing their tiny two-bedroom apartment, and soon they'd need more space and a yard for Cynthia to play. All they had now was a pad of cement in back of the brownstone. When spring came, Louise expected to spend a lot of time pushing her daughter's buggy back and forth to the nearest park.

"I'll scramble an egg for you as soon as I put this last batch in," Louise said, peering into the oven to see if a pan was ready to take out.

"No hurry," Eliot said. "I'll take a bath and shave first so you have more time to finish. Did you get any sleep last night? I must have slept through the feedings."

"Enough to get by on," Louise assured him, although she felt bone-weary.

With her small kitchen counter covered with cooling cookies, Louise used her last egg to make her husband's breakfast. Fortunately, she was satisfied with a bowl of corn flakes for herself. In fact, she was too tired to bother with eating, but Eliot would be concerned if she didn't join him for the morning meal. They'd always enjoyed talking over their plans for the day before he had to leave for work.

"I'm going to Wanamaker's to buy material this afternoon," she said. "Maxine agreed to watch Cynthia. She's the only person I'd trust to watch our baby, at least in Philadelphia."

Eliot put down his toast and raised his eyebrows. "Is it really necessary to go that far for a piece of cloth?"

Her husband was rarely critical, and Louise knew it was a fair question. The round-trip bus ride and the higher prices at the huge department store were expenses they didn't need, but he didn't understand how important the stocking was.

"I've already checked every place close by. I wouldn't make the trip if I could find something special closer to home," she said.

"I still think Cynthia could wait until next Christmas," he said mildly. It was as close to criticism as he ever got.

"It's important to me, as a way to honor my mother," she said in a quiet voice.

The last thing she wanted was to add to their financial woes, but she was always careful with money. Her parents had lived a frugal life on a minister's pay, but her mother had still managed to carry on the family's Christmas traditions, even when she had two daughters and a third on the way. Louise didn't see how she could do less.

Eliot nodded and said no more, but Louise could sense his concerns.

"I've saved up enough from the birthday money my father gave me," she said, not adding that she'd also been very frugal in her grocery shopping.

It was an uncomfortable feeling, not being totally honest with Eliot. They both had been forthcoming throughout their court-ship and marriage so far, but she had saved her birthday money to spend as she liked. After buying a nice sweater vest for Eliot's Christmas gift, she had a bit left. As tired as she was, she was deter-mined to do the things her mother had done for her daughters.

Her friendly neighbor tapped on the door at exactly 2:00 PM, as promised. Maxine was a young, unmarried nurse who worked different hours every week. Fortunately, she was on the night shift today.

"I can't tell you how much I appreciate this," Louise said to the pretty dark-haired woman. "I promise not to be gone any lon-ger than necessary."

"You don't need to hurry back," her friend said. "I've been dying to spend time with your beautiful daughter. I went into nursing because I love babies, but so far the hospital has me work-ing with adult surgery patients. I'm still hoping for an assignment in the newborn nursery."

Cynthia made her presence known with a loud wail, making it hard for her mother to leave.

"I'll get her," Maxine said. "You run along. Baby Cynthia will be fine."

"I wrote down her schedule and where to find everything."

"Great. Thank you."

"And here's the number of her pediatrician, just in case—"

"We'll manage," Maxine said with a broad smile. "I have a feeling Cynthia will make her needs known."

"Undoubtedly," Louise said. As much as Louise wanted to shop for material, she was finding it hard to actually walk out the door. "This is the first time I've left her with anyone but my husband," she said, forcing a weak smile.

"We'll be right here when you get back."

After one more loving glance at her daughter, Louise hurried out into the frigid air. The bus stop was only a few blocks away, but she was thoroughly chilled by the time the bus came, spewing out exhaust that made her wrinkle her nose. At least the interior was warm, and she took one of the many worn leather seats available at this time of day. She did hope she wouldn't have to ride home standing and hanging onto one of the straps. Maybe if she hurried with her shopping, she could still beat the after-work crush.

At least she was able to exit the bus close to the store's entrance. Even though the department store had lost some of its early grandeur, she still enjoyed going in through the Grand Court, where a huge bronze eagle had become a city icon. If she weren't in a hurry and strapped for cash, she would've loved to have a hot chocolate in the Crystal Tea Room. Unfortunately, she didn't have time to admire the Renaissance décor or wander the many departments.

She made her way to the yard goods section. The cloth on display didn't disappoint. In fact, there were so many choices, Louise wasn't sure where to look first. She wandered through the rows of fabric displayed on bolts, stopping to admire some especially lovely brocades laced with gold threads. The material was too heavy for Cynthia's stocking, but it was a pleasure to see it.

A whole aisle was devoted to Christmas fabrics, including some quilted patterns, but Louise changed her mind about using one of them when she saw a lovely crimson velvet.

"Isn't this delightful," a stout woman said as she fingered the fabric that had caught Louise's eye. "But I guess my husband would rather have a nice wool for the robe I'm making him for Christmas."

Louise was glad the other woman passed up the red velvet. She picked up the bolt to carry it to the long table where clerks cut the cloth to size, but first she needed a different fabric for the lining. She found it as soon as she walked down the next aisle. A beautiful forest-green satin caught her eye, and she knew it would be perfect.

Both fabrics were pricey, but at least matching thread wasn't. Louise had to do some mental arithmetic to be sure she had enough money. Fortunately, she could pay for everything and still have bus money to get home. She waited behind several other customers for her turn, but finally she had exactly the right fabric in a distinctive Wanamaker's shopping bag.

On the bus ride home, she was fortunate to snag a seat. Hugging her purse and her purchases against her chest, she felt drowsiness catch up with her. She closed her eyes to rest them for a minute.

The woman in the window seat excused herself and stepped over Louise's feet, doing her a big favor by waking her just blocks from her stop. She hadn't even noticed when the bus stopped for more passengers, and there were a lot of people hanging from straps on the lurching vehicle. She stood and weaved her way through the standing riders, clasping at seat backs to keep her balance, to make sure she didn't miss getting off at the right place.

When she got back to the apartment, Maxine was rocking a contented baby, but she was quick to mention Cynthia's colic.

"She was cranky, but she finally calmed down. At least it gave me an excuse to keep holding her," Maxine said.

Louise's arms ached to hold her, but first she had to take off her coat and show the beautiful fabric to her friend.

"This is really special," Maxine agreed. "Will it be hard to sew? I'm not very good at using my mother's machine."

Louise hadn't given that any thought. She had only thought about making a beautiful Christmas stocking her daughter would always cherish, just as Louise did with the one her mother had made for her.

"I guess I'll have to be very careful with it," Louise said before profusely thanking her friend.

"Oh, your minister dropped off a folder of music for you," she said as she surrendered Cynthia and began putting on her coat.

"You don't have to thank me. I adore your baby. Call me anytime you need someone to watch her."

Her friend left, and Cynthia was sleeping contentedly in her crib. Louise's fingers itched to begin sewing, but she'd been gone longer than expected. Eliot would be home soon, and she had to come up with something for his supper before she left for the first concert rehearsal. She frantically checked her refrigerator and cupboard, but the best she could do in a hurry was open a can of tomato soup and make sandwiches. The frosting on the cookies had been drying all afternoon, and she needed to store the decorated cookies in the tin cans she'd saved for that purpose, and she still needed to look over the selections for the concert.

How did her mother make Christmas perfect with so many demands on her time? Louise didn't know, but she was still determined to follow in her footsteps.

Heavy gray clouds hung over the city like smoke from a massive bonfire. Peeking up at the sky from her kitchen window, Louise hoped it wouldn't snow until she got home from the concert rehearsal. Their aging two-door sedan was fine for getting Eliot to and from work, but she didn't trust it when she was driving in bad weather.

"I'm home." Her husband called out the most welcome words of the day as he came into the apartment. "How are my little women?"

He said the same thing every time he came home, but Louise loved to hear it. And, thankfully, he said it quietly enough not to wake Cynthia, who was finally napping.

"She's sleeping, bless her heart," Louise said, taking her husband's worn gabardine overcoat and hanging it up for him. He never expected her to wait on him, but she loved doing little things for him.

"How was your day?" he asked, walking to the kitchenette, where she had hastily assembled a meal of canned tomato soup and ham sandwiches on pumpernickel bread.

"Maxine watched Cynthia. She was fussy—the baby, not Maxine—but now she's sleeping soundly. I hope she'll be good for you while I'm at the rehearsal."

"We'll be fine," Eliot assured her, knowing she worried every time the baby was out of her sight.

"I bought the most beautiful material," Louise said, taking the bag off the table to show him.

"Very nice," he said, hardly glancing at it.

She didn't expect him to share her appreciation of the fabric, but she'd hoped for a little more enthusiasm.

"You don't like it."

"Of course, I do," he was quick to say. "I'm just afraid you're taking on too much, especially since you agreed to take over the concert."

My mother could do more than this, Louise thought, but she didn't want to argue the point with her husband.

Cynthia woke up with indignant howls before they finished dinner, but Eliot volunteered to take care of her so Louise could get ready to leave. Before she could change into her blue wool skirt and white pullover sweater, he had to call on her for help with a bottle.

"The nipple doesn't seem to be working," he said. He sounded frustrated, and Louise knew it was because their daughter wasn't patient about waiting when she was hungry.

"I sterilized extra," Louise said. "Just switch them."

By the time Cynthia was happy with her bottle, Louise had to leave. She would've liked time to do her hair with the curling iron and then put on makeup, but it was more important to get to the church a few minutes early. She always felt more organized if she didn't rush in at the last minute.

Fortunately, the snow held off, although the wind was bitterly cold, cutting through her good navy wool coat and chilling her to the bone. The custodian had left the lights and heat on for the rehearsal, but she kept her coat on until she felt warm.

The comfortable quiet in the sanctuary invited a few moments of silent prayer in a front pew. Louise knew how much she had to be grateful for, especially her loving husband and beautiful new daughter. The words of her prayer came easily, interrupted after a brief interlude by the arrival of the pianist for the concert.

"Louise, I'm so glad you agreed to direct the concert," Mary Grogan said, vigorously rubbing her slender hands together to warm them.

"It's a privilege and a pleasure," Louise said. "Thank heavens you're accompanying on the piano."

She genuinely admired the tall, thin, older woman, although she had a reputation for being eccentric. Louise knew it was mainly due to the way she dressed, which mostly included black, black and more black.

"How do you like the selections?" Mary asked, arranging her music on the piano.

"I'm pleased, especially with 'Lo, How a Rose 'ere Blooming.' It's not usually included in Christmas programs."

"You and I know it's an advent hymn," Mary said with a smile, "but it's a wonderful addition to the program."

Several choir members came into the church together, and others soon followed. Louise felt a bit intimidated to be directing people who had much more experience than she did, but music had always been very important to her. It had brought Eliot and her together when she was his student, and she couldn't imagine a time when it wasn't a major part of her life.

"I'm sorry Mrs. Taylor was injured in a fall," Louise said when everyone had arrived. "She has a broken arm, and there's no possibility she'll be able to direct the concert. For those who don't know me, I'm Louise Smith. I'll do my best to carry on, although I don't pretend I can take her place."

"We're very happy to have you," a woman named Naomi said, echoed by several other voices.

Once they got into the rehearsal, Louise's nervousness passed. Although she wished there'd been more time to prepare, she was reasonably satisfied with the way things went until one of the sopranos started coughing so hard she couldn't continue. Several other choir members coughed from time to time, and Louise began to worry about the health of the participants. What would happen to the concert if a flu epidemic hit the group?

"We'll follow the schedule Mrs. Taylor made," Louise said when the rehearsal was over. "I hope you'll all pray to stay healthy. If your throats are a little raspy, you might try hot tea with lemon and honey when you get home. Thank you so much for coming."

Louise had to wait until everyone left before turning out the lights and locking the side door the choir members used. Mary left with her so they could walk to their cars together. Thankfully the pianist hadn't been coughing during the rehearsal.

"I hope you stay healthy," Louise said. "I don't think I can direct *and* play the piano."

"Let's hope you won't have to," Mary said, unlocking her car, which was parked next to Louise's. "And thank you again for taking over."

Hard pellets of icy snow hit the windshield as Louise drove home, and their snug little apartment had never seemed more welcoming. She came in with her head scarf and coat damp and her fingers stiff from the cold. The heater in their car didn't work very well, but they'd been avoiding a potentially costly trip to the garage.

Eliot was pacing the floor with a sleeping baby, but his face was lined with weariness.

"How did it go?" he asked, gingerly carrying Cynthia to her crib.

"Fine, except a soprano had a coughing fit, and several others seemed to be having trouble too. Fortunately, it's a large choir. We'll be okay if not too many people get sick."

"I've had a few students down with the flu," Eliot said. "Hope it's not an epidemic. It's not a good sign the papers have given it a name: Asian flu. Says it hit last it in the late 1950s."

"How was Cynthia?" Louise shook out her coat before hanging it up.

"She cried most of the evening."

"You look exhausted. Why don't you go to bed?"

"Good idea. I have one more exam to give in the morning, and I'm not done correcting the last one. Come join me before our precious little soprano wakes up again."

"I want to cut out the stocking first. If I do a little at a time, it will be done by Christmas," Louise said.

Eliot sighed, a strong sign of disapproval for him.

"Tomorrow is another day," he said.

"I won't be long. I'll just lay out the material and pin on the pattern I've already drawn. You go ahead."

Before he could leave their living area, Cynthia started whimpering, building up to a loud howl before Louise could pick her up.

"When did you last feed her?" she asked.

"When you left. Do you want me to handle this one?"

He sounded so weary Louise didn't even consider his offer.

"No, go to bed. I had a little nap." She didn't mention it happened by accident on the bus ride home.

Louise picked up her baby and managed to warm the bottle in a pan of water using her free hand. She changed her just in case she nodded off after eating.

Lots of things about caring for a new baby were deeply satisfying, but the biggest challenge was staying awake while her infant dawdled over her bottle. Louise was afraid of falling asleep and dropping Cynthia, so instead of contentedly rocking her, she ended up pacing and feeding her at the same time.

"Rock-a-bye baby," Louise sang softly, but the lovely old lullaby did nothing to put her daughter to sleep. After what seemed like hours—but was less than forty-five minutes on the kitchen clock—Cynthia finally surrendered to sleep. Her tiny lids drooped, then closed, and the serene beauty of her face tugged at Louise's heartstrings. She gently laid her down in her cradle.

The lovely material was still in the sack on the table. She took it out and fingered the luxurious velvet. It was wonderfully soft, but it still couldn't compare to the feel of her daughter's downy head against her cheek.

One way or another, Cynthia was going to have a beautiful stocking for her first Christmas. But maybe it wasn't a good idea to start cutting this late at night.

Louise gave in to her fatigue and went to prepare for the night. She was tired from the top of her head to the bottom of her feet. Tomorrow was another day, and maybe her baby would give her the great gift of a good night's sleep.

How had her mother managed to do all she did with two small daughters? Reeling with fatigue, Louise made quick work of getting ready for bed. The pillow under her cheek was cool and welcoming, and oblivion swiftly overcame her.

How much sleep did a colicky baby need? Apparently less than her mother, Louise thought as she slid her legs over the edge of the bed and groped for her slippers with her feet. She was almost afraid to look at the clock. This was the second time Cynthia had cried in the night, and it was only a little after 6:00 AM.

At least there was one good thing about waking up that early. She would have a long day to work on the stocking. Surely a baby as young as her daughter would have to sleep sometime.

"What time is it?" Eliot mumbled, still half asleep.

"Early," Louise said, standing to find her robe. "Go back to sleep. You have to give an exam this morning."

When she picked up her daughter, it was immediately obvious her diaper had leaked. The pail Louise used to soak the diapers was nearly full, and somehow she had to make time to do laundry in the washing machine in the basement. The landlord supplied an old wringer washer, but there wasn't a dryer. Louise either had to hang everything on lines strung across the laundry area or haul everything to the Laundromat.

Maybe she could wash a few things in the sink, enough to last until the weekend, when Eliot could watch Cynthia. They would dry fairly fast if she hung them over the old-fashioned steam radiator. The basement was too musty and damp for a baby, and she wouldn't bring her out in the frigid weather even if her husband left the car and took the bus to work.

"What you need is a bath," Louise cooed to her daughter.

Unfortunately, she didn't have the energy to go through the complicated process of setting up the plastic tub on the sink drain board at this hour of the day. Anyway, the apartment was too cold and probably wouldn't warm up until midmorning. She quickly changed every stitch on her baby and stripped off the wet blankets and sheets. She wanted to scrub the plastic pad before replacing them, but first it sounded like Cynthia's tiny tummy was ready for formula. Louise mentally calculated the supply in the fridge and knew sterilizing a new load of bottles was a top priority.

It was noon before all her essential jobs were done. She looked longingly at the fabric she'd spread out on a card table in the living area. Cynthia was awake and happily cooing in her little seat, and there was only one more thing Louise had to do before working on the stocking. Lately her meals had been sketchy at best, but Eliot hadn't complained. Tonight she wanted to prepare something he liked: hunter's stew. It was made with ground beef, potatoes, carrots, onions, and canned peas, all blended together with creamed corn. She could make it now and warm it when he got home, since the flavor only improved if it sat a while.

After cutting up the vegetables, she browned the meat and added it, stirring with a watchful eye on Cynthia. When the ingredients were cooked through, she added a can of creamed corn and took the pan from the stove. Scooping it into a ceramic bowl, she refrigerated it next to the newly prepared formula, happy to have a nice meal she could serve quickly.

Cynthia was making little noises that Louise interpreted as signs of hunger. It was one of God's miracles that a baby could communicate its needs without words. She hurried to warm a bottle, hoping this feeding would go well.

Settled down in the rocker with her baby wrapped in a soft flannel blanket, Louise marveled at the sheer joy of holding her child. Cynthia drank eagerly for a minute or so, then began toying with the bottle. It was impossible to know whether she was full or just tired of sucking, but Louise knew if she didn't take more than a scant ounce, she'd be hungry again in less than an hour.

Sometimes it helped to sing. Louise softly cooed a lullaby, but it didn't encourage Cynthia to drink the small amount in her bottle any faster. When at last she'd drained all but the last half ounce, Louise changed her and put her down for a nap, hoping for a couple of hours to work on the stocking.

As soon as she'd spread out the velvet, Cynthia dashed her hopes for a quiet work session. Her hysterical cries shattered the peace in the apartment, and Louise hurried to pick her up, gently patting her back in hopes of relieving another bout of colic.

Cynthia wasn't easily pacified. Louise paced within the confines of the apartment until even her lightweight daughter seemed heavy. She sang, hummed, and cooed some more, all to no avail, gently rubbing and patting her baby's back the whole time.

When, at last, Cynthia relaxed in sleep, Louise carefully laid her down. She felt groggy with fatigue, unable to remember when she'd last had a good night's sleep. Maybe if she took a very short nap, she'd awake alert and refreshed.

Rather than lie on her bed, she hunkered down on their lumpy secondhand couch, sure she wouldn't sleep long if she wasn't comfortable. She pulled an old afghan her grandmother had made years and years ago up to her chin and dropped off to sleep immediately.

The next thing she knew, Eliot was standing over her, still wearing his coat and gloves.

"Sorry, I didn't mean to wake you," he said.

"What time is it?" She sat up with alarm, hardly able to believe she'd slept until he got home.

"Not quite five thirty. Did you have a good nap?"

"Too good," she said, quickly rising. "I have to check on Cynthia."

"I just did. She's sound asleep." He took off his coat and hung it up. "I'm really glad you got some rest, especially since you have another rehearsal tonight."

"Oh dear, I shouldn't have slept so long. It's past time to feed Cynthia, and I have to warm the stew for supper."

"I'm sure she'll let you know when she's hungry, and I'll warm supper so you can get ready for the rehearsal."

He went to the kitchenette and opened the refrigerator. "Looks like my favorite, hunter's stew. You make it even better than my mother did when I was a kid."

"I'll turn it on high and stir it so it won't burn," she said. "You can help by setting the table. With any luck, we can eat before Cynthia wakes up. Poor little thing must be exhausted."

Eliot turned on the tiny radio they kept on the counter, keeping the sound low. "Let's get some news. I haven't had time to buy a paper this week."

Although her interest in the news broadcast was low, Louise couldn't help but hear the words 'Asian flu.'

"What was that about the flu?" she asked.

"Only that several public schools have closed early this week because so many pupils and faculty are out sick," he said seriously. "I'm glad our students are having their winter break now."

When the broadcast was over, he turned it off and took his place at the table. Louise filled a bowl with the stew and put a plate of saltine crackers on the table.

They took turns saying a blessing, but Louise liked it best when Eliot did it. He never used a traditional prayer, but always made one up. This evening he asked the Lord's blessing for the recovery of the many flu victims.

Although the stew wasn't her favorite, Louise ate with a hearty appetite for the first time in weeks. Apparently a long nap made food taste better.

"I thought I'd have time to feed Cynthia before the rehearsal," she said after quietly checking on her sleeping baby.

"I'll take care of it. And I'll wash the supper dishes. The streets are a little slick, so you should get an early start and drive slowly."

"I'll get home as soon as possible. I know you have grading to do." They often mused that teachers had more homework than their students.

Grateful for his help, Louise quickly changed clothes and left for the church, wondering as she drove whether any choir members would be out sick.

Much to her relief, her pianist was there before her.

"It's chilly in here," Mary Grogan said, still wearing her winter coat as she warmed her fingers by playing scales.

"Maybe it will feel warmer when everyone gets here," Louise said, although she wasn't optimistic. It was a large church, and the rows of dark wooden pews that contrasted so beautifully with the cream-colored wall in daylight looked stark in the yellow light of the ceiling fixtures high above them.

"The Butlers called me—they weren't sure about your number because there are quite a few Smiths in the phone directory," Mary said. "They're both down with the flu. Gerald said his wife can hardly lift her head off the pillow. I haven't heard how long this Asian flu lasts. Have you?"

"No," Louise said. "I do hope it won't go through the whole choir. It would be such a shame to cancel the concert."

"Yes, I can remember playing it for at least fifteen years, and it was an important tradition long before we moved here and joined the church."

"Well, maybe they're the only ones who are sick," Louise said without too much hope, making a mental note not to get too close to anyone who was coughing. It would be a nightmare if she got sick and brought it home to Cynthia and Eliot. Fortunately, neither she nor her husband were very vulnerable to viruses.

The rehearsal wasn't a disaster, but it was disappointing to see that three other people were home sick. One of their soloists had to leave the sanctuary because she was coughing too much to sing, but the rest of the choir really threw themselves into the music to make up for the missing members.

"If there aren't any more people down sick, we should be okay," Mary said when everyone else had left. "I think Harriet can do the solo if Ginny is ill. But I don't think coughing is a sign of the flu, at least from what I've heard. Maybe she just has a cold."

"Let's hope she'll be over it soon. We only have a week until the concert," Louise said as much to herself as Mary. "I pray the epidemic will stop soon," Louise said.

"Yes, apparently it's very dangerous for the elderly. We might not have the large attendance the Christmas concert usually gets," Mary said.

"That would be a shame. The choir really sounds lovely, and they couldn't have a better accompanist." Louise gratefully pulled on her coat and gloves, making a mental note to wear two sweaters to the next rehearsal. A person really couldn't direct wearing a winter coat.

"I'll see you Monday evening for the next rehearsal," Mary said, slipping into her black coat.

"Yes, Monday," Louise said. "Thanks for all you're doing."

At least she would have the next evening free to work on the stocking. She turned off the lights and locked the door, wondering why she still felt weary after her long nap. Having a baby seemed to take the starch out of a person.

When she got home, Louise found Eliot still at work, his grading materials spread out on the kitchen table.

"I'm later than I thought," she said apologetically. "How is the grading going?"

"Slowly, I'm afraid. Cynthia woke up cranky as soon as you left. I guess she missed her mother because she cried most of the evening."

"I'm sorry," Louise said. "We had to work extra hard because several choir members are down with the flu. At least tomorrow is Friday, so there's no rehearsal."

"How's it going?" he asked.

"Okay. One soloist has a cough, but I guess that's not a symptom of this new flu. I hope she'll be able to sing at the concert. She has a week to get over it. I have a substitute in mind, but she's not nearly as good."

"I think I'll call it a night," her husband said, standing and stretching. "If I get up early, I can still make the deadline for turning in grades. Let's go to bed before Cynthia wakes up again."

"You go ahead. I'll be along in a while." With both her husband and baby sleeping, she could finally get started on the stocking.

"You really should get some sleep while you can," Eliot said. "You look absolutely exhausted."

"You're right, I'm sure, but this is the first chance I've had to begin work on Cynthia's Christmas stocking. I'll only work a little while."

"It can wait," her husband insisted. "Your health is more important than a stocking, and you look beat. What possible difference can it make if it isn't done until next Christmas?"

Louise tried to stifle her irritation, but it wasn't like Eliot to be so closed-minded. Why couldn't he see how important it was to follow in her mother's footsteps? She would be devastated if she couldn't finish the stocking for Cynthia's first Christmas. She even had a few little presents to put in it: a new rattle, a pretty embroidered bib, and the cutest red and white striped stockings with tassels. Even before the baby was born, she'd tucked away a few small purchases so Cynthia would have presents to celebrate the Lord's birth.

"I don't want to wait," she said emphatically.

"Very well. I'm going to bed." He squared his shoulders and left the room without saying good night.

Eliot was slow to anger, and they'd never had a real fight. In fact, they rarely disagreed on anything important. This was the exception. Louise was beside herself, frustrated because he couldn't or wouldn't see how important Christmas traditions were in her family.

His family had their own holiday customs, but they'd seemed to lose importance after his parents moved to Florida to retire. There was something about lazing on the beach on Christmas Day that didn't appeal at all to Louise, but she respected what they wanted to do. Why couldn't her husband make an effort to understand why she needed to follow her mother's traditions?

After making a cup of tea, she settled down at the folding table, taking the velvet and satin out of the department store bag. Her eyes were tired, but she still loved the sight of the deep red and shimmering green fabric. She'd made her own paper pattern, really just an enlargement of one she'd seen in a women's magazine, because she wanted it large enough to hold gifts, not just hang as decoration.

For a few moments she imagined her little girl as a toddler, old enough to pull packages and sweet treats out of her stocking. When would she start talking? How old were babies when they said their first word?

Louise forgot about her husband's objections and daydreamed about the wonderful years to come. When should she start teaching Cynthia to play the piano? Of course, first they'd have to buy one, and that meant having a home large enough to accommodate it. Maybe someday her little darling would have a grand piano, but she'd have to begin on an inexpensive upright.

In fact, Louise looked forward to having pupils besides her daughter. They could use the extra income, and she loved introducing children to the wonderful world of music.

"Oh my, I'm going to nod off if I don't get to work," she said to herself. Woolgathering wasn't going to get the stocking cut out.

Since her time was so limited, she wondered if it was possible to cut both pieces of material at the same time. All she'd have to do was carefully pin them together, then pin the pattern onto both layers. It would be quicker, and the lining and outer fabric would be exactly the same size.

After spreading out the satin and smoothing it down, she laid the velvet on top. Both pieces of cloth were so lovely, it was almost a shame to cut into them. But, of course, the completed stocking would be even more beautiful.

Louise hoped that their house, when they bought one, would have a fireplace. It wasn't right to tack a Christmas stocking any old place, and hanging it on a doorknob was even less appealing. When they started looking for a permanent home, she was going to put a fireplace at the top of the list, followed closely by room for a piano. And, of course, Cynthia had to have safe places to play, both inside and out.

Her eyelids were drooping, and she realized she was close to nodding off. It was so pleasant to imagine her baby growing up in a home with room for all three of them to pursue their interests. Eliot, bless his heart, was a good sport about working on the kitchen table, but he really did need a quiet corner with a desk and bookcases. With any luck, they could find a house with a spare bedroom to convert into an office for him.

She shook her head to stay awake and sipped the tea she'd allowed to grow cold. In fact, the apartment was quickly losing heat, and she tiptoed to look at Cynthia in her bed to be sure she was still covered.

"Sleep well, my dearest daughter," she murmured, silently hurrying back to her worktable.

For some reason she'd inherited her mother's workbox, although both Alice and Jane were more likely to sew. She took out the big, heavy scissors, older than she was but still wonderfully sharp, and made a small, tentative cut. The blades of the shears cut through the double layer of fabric like a knife through butter, and Louise was encouraged to continue.

Her fingers seemed to have a will of their own, guiding the heavy blades through the ultrasoft material. Velvet, she was learning, had a will of its own, and she could feel the satin under it sliding around. She checked to be sure the cuts were going through both layers, but it took some maneuvering to keep the two slippery pieces in place. She was beginning to doubt the wisdom of cutting both together. Worse, maybe Eliot was right: She should have gone to bed and left the stocking for another day. But with only a little over a week left until Christmas, could she depend on her colicky daughter to sleep enough to let her complete it?

Her mind had wandered again, much to her distress. This wasn't an easy project, especially for someone who usually limited her sewing to buttons and hems.

The first side of the stocking was ready to unpin, but as soon as she separated the two layers, Louise was devastated. Somehow the velvet had puckered, and the side opposite the salvage was a full inch shorter than it should have been. The satin had crinkled up, and the foot part was much too narrow.

"Have I ruined it?" she asked herself with alarm.

Perhaps it would still work, but she obviously had to cut the materials separately. She felt groggy from fatigue, but this had to be done. Repeating the process of pinning and cutting, she finally had four pieces to work with. The full extent of her mistakes hit as soon as she lined up the pieces next to each other. The pins had put something like a runner down the middle of the satin, and the first piece definitely wasn't big enough to be the lining.

Her first thought was to make the stocking without a lining, but the slippery material had betrayed her. The two pieces were so mismatched, they wouldn't be suitable for a stocking half the size she'd planned.

Hot, wet tears coursed down her cheeks before she even realized she was crying. After all the trouble and expense of getting the perfect fabric, all she had was a pile of badly cut remnants. She just wasn't good at sewing. Her mother had made sewing look easy, but for Louise it was the Mount Everest of homemaking.

She put her head down on the table like a kindergartner at rest time and sobbed until sleep overcame her.

Crying penetrated her dream, and she woke up to see Eliot standing over her with a sobbing Cynthia on his shoulder.

"Wake up, darling. You need to go to bed."

"The baby. . ."

"I'll feed her," he said in a soft voice. "You'd better get some sleep in a bed."

"Oh, Eliot," she said, remembering the mess she'd made of the fabric, "I ruined the fabric. It was so expensive, and I cut it all wrong."

"It will be all right. You can get more material," he reassured her. "Use the change in the coffee tin."

"We were saving that for new tires," she protested.

"Ours will last another year. After all, we only drive the car in town. Go pick out something nice tomorrow, but tonight it's time to get some sleep."

She hugged him and the baby and staggered off to bed, too tired to bother with her bedtime routine. When Eliot crawled in beside her, she was only vaguely aware of it. The next thing she knew, the weak winter sun was peeping around the edges of the curtains, and her husband was gone.

In the kitchen, she found a brief note on the counter: "Fed Cynthia at 5:30. Hope you can catch up on your sleep. Use the tire money to replace the material. Love to both my girls."

He didn't have to sign it. She only wished he was there so she could tell him how much she loved him.

Friday morning Louise awoke feeling more upbeat until she remembered the ruined fabric. Somehow she had to find a replacement, but there was no way she had the time or the money for another trip to the center of the city.

Fortunately, Eliot would be home at noon to begin his winter break. If she knew her husband, he'd still spend time working in his office on campus. Students might take vacations, but their teachers had lots of work to do to get ready for the next semester.

"Good morning, sleepyhead," he said, coming into their bedroom fully dressed.

"What time is it?" Louise asked, peering at the alarm clock beside their bed.

"Time for me to get to work, but I'll be home by noon."

"Cynthia—"

"Has a full tummy and a dry diaper. She's actually awake and happy for the moment." He leaned over and kissed her as she sat on the edge of the bed.

"You're a wonderful man," Louise said with feeling. "You let me sleep while you took care of her."

"You needed a full night. Anyway, it's a joy to hold our daughter in my arms, especially when she isn't howling like a banshee. And I am sorry about your material. But maybe you should wait until next year. By then Cynthia should be sleeping through the night."

"Next year?" Louise stood. "I'm making a stocking for her first Christmas."

"Louise, give yourself a break. There's no deadline on doing something nice for the baby. She won't know the difference."

"That's not the point." Louise despaired of making him understand the importance of her mother's tradition. "As soon as you get home with the car, I'm going shopping. You did say I could use some of the change we saved up for tires."

"Yes, of course you can. It's not the cost of a little material I'm worried about. It's the pressure you're putting on yourself. Isn't the concert enough to keep you occupied in the little spare time you have?"

Louise clamped her lips shut. They so rarely argued about anything that she didn't know how to react. For a moment she worried that she was being too stubborn. But Eliot hadn't lost his mother when he was young. He didn't understand how much Louise had missed not being able to show her lovely daughter to her maternal grandmother. Her father had come to see Cynthia shortly after her birth, but his joy only made Louise mourn the loss of her mother more. She was determined to honor her mother's traditions in observing the birth of the Savior.

"I'll see you around noon," Eliot said, leaving the room to put on his coat.

After slipping into her quilted blue robe, she sat on the edge of the bed until the door closed after him. The stocking wasn't anything to argue about. She was going to make one, and that was that.

The morning went quickly. Cynthia cooed during her bath, and Louise was almost sure she'd smiled, never mind that the pediatrician said it was only gas. She even managed to take a bath herself while the baby napped, although laundry was piling up.

"I'm home," Eliot called out a little after noon. "How are my little women?"

"I left a bologna sandwich in the fridge for your lunch, and there are carrot strips to go with it," Louise said, rushing to leave. "I only took a little tire money, so you don't need to worry about the stocking costing too much."

"I wasn't," her husband said, pursing his lips in irritation. "It's you I'm worried about. It would be much better if you took a little nap before the faculty Christmas party tonight."

Louise stopped short with one arm thrust into her coat.

"The faculty party," she said with dismay, hardly able to believe she'd forgotten all about it.

"Don't tell me it slipped your mind," Eliot said as she nodded. "You really do need to get more sleep. It's totally unlike you not to remember. You even made cookies for it."

"It's Friday, isn't it?" She felt like a bad wife, even though she knew her husband was the most understanding of men. "My days have blurred together."

"You have a sitter lined up, don't you?" he asked mildly.

"Oh dear."

"You don't?"

"No, but I'll call Maxine right now. If she can't come, I might not be able to go with you."

He looked so unhappy at the prospect of going alone that her guilt doubled. She threw her coat on the couch and hurried to make the call.

"As luck would have it," Maxine said, "I had a date, but he came down with Asian flu. I'll be happy to watch Cynthia."

Louise hurried to tell Eliot the good news and apologized profusely for forgetting.

"Louise, you expect yourself to be perfect, and no one is," he said in a loving voice.

"I'll set out your lunch before I go," she said, not wavering in her determination to buy new fabric.

"I wish you'd use the tire money to buy yourself a pretty new dress," he said as he sat at the table. "You haven't had one in ages."

"That's because I was pregnant," she was quick to point out. "But I can still get into my blue jersey, and it will look nice with the silver necklace you gave me last Christmas."

He shook his head indulgently. "You're beautiful, no matter what you wear, but I still wish you'd do something nice for yourself instead of worrying about a stocking our daughter won't even notice yet."

That was her cue to leave, and she did so without further comment. She loved her handsome husband with all her heart, but today he was annoying her.

Even with the car and a fair amount of tire money, all in change, she didn't want to go far from home. Her best bet was a small shopping area a couple of miles from their apartment, but the selection there was disappointing. Two elderly sisters owned the shop, which sold everything from bulk candy to bedroom slippers. In fact, Louise couldn't figure out exactly what kind of store it was, but they did have a few bolts of material in a back corner.

Fortunately, the sisters had stocked up on Christmas prints. Unfortunately, they were mundane compared to the gorgeous fabric Louise had ruined. It didn't take long to make up her mind. There was really only one she considered worthy of her daughter's stocking. It was a red quilted material with a Christmas tree pattern. Toys were scattered throughout the design, and although she wanted Christmas to mean more than gifts to her daughter, it would have to do. The best thing was she wouldn't have to line it.

Mildred, the older sister, cut the fabric with the precision of an engineer, cutting it so slowly Louise want to grab the scissors from her and finish the job herself.

"Isn't this the cutest pattern you've ever seen?" the plump little shopkeeper asked. "If it doesn't all sell, I think I'll make some potholders for my brother's family. He has four grown children and seven grandchildren. Maud and I never married, you know, but we've enjoyed our nieces and nephews so much."

Louise smiled and made polite conversation, but inside she was seething with impatience, so much so that she hardly recognized herself. Was this what they called postpartum blues? If so, she had a raging case. At least it wasn't the flu.

When she got home, Eliot was walking the floor with Cynthia, unsuccessfully trying to quiet her.

"You look exhausted," Louise said, remembering how he'd let her sleep as late as possible. "Take a nap. You'll enjoy the party more if you do."

For once he didn't try to be noble and refuse. "Thanks, I think I will," he said. "Can the laundry wait until tomorrow? I'll take it to the Laundromat so we don't have to hang it in the musty basement."

He didn't ask to see her fabric, even though the sisters' flaming pink shopping bag was too obvious to overlook.

In spite of her best intentions, the afternoon flew by without an opportunity to take the cloth out of the shop's sack. She tried hard to keep Cynthia quiet so Eliot could get some much-needed sleep. It was nearly five when he woke up, and she had yet to give any thought to supper.

"None for me, I think," he said when she asked what he'd like. "They always have enough appetizers to more than make up for a missed meal. It's the only chance I get to eat my fill of things like shrimp and fondue."

Somehow Louise had forgotten to eat lunch, so she had a quick bowl of cornflakes to hold her over until the party. By the time Maxine arrived, she felt somewhat festive in her favorite dressy dress, although a trip to the beauty parlor would've been nice.

Even though she'd been to a number of faculty gatherings with Eliot, she was always a little edgy at their parties. It was hard to forget that some of the partygoers had been her instructors not too many years before. She tried to appear poised and confident, but inside she was a churning mass of nerves as they made their entrance.

Fortunately, she'd worried for nothing. Several of the younger faculty wives took her in tow, and she enjoyed their conversation, especially comparing notes on their babies.

"My Sally finally slept through the night," a pretty brunette mother said. "I thought they'd have to put me in a room with padded walls if I didn't get a night's sleep soon."

When the party was over, Louise felt more relaxed than she had in a long time. She wasn't the only mother struggling with a colicky baby and the busy Christmas season.

"Did you enjoy yourself?" Eliot asked on their way home.

"Yes, I did," she admitted. "After Christmas I may get together with a couple of other new mothers. It would be nice to share our experiences."

When they got home, she wasn't surprised to see Maxine rocking the baby.

"Was she terribly fussy?" Louise asked with concern.

"Let's just say I didn't have time to open the book I brought," her friend said. "But it's fun to spend an evening with your darling daughter."

Maxine always refused payment, but Louise made a mental note to do something nice for her in the future. By the time they'd said good-bye, Eliot had put Cynthia down for the night and was in the bedroom getting ready for bed himself.

"Coming, sweetheart?" he asked, appearing in the open door in his pajamas.

"I just want to lay out the material first. Get a head start on tomorrow."

"Working late at night didn't work out so well yesterday." He said it in a kind tone, but it hurt to be reminded of the way she'd ruined the lovely velvet and satin.

Much as she hated to admit it, he was probably right. She wasn't very good at sewing, and the quilted material could pose some problems. At least she had the weekend to work on it. Certainly she'd have time then to make a very nice Christmas stocking.

Louise knew she had to get up Saturday morning, but her eyes felt stuck shut. As far as she could remember, Cynthia had slept in two-hour blocks of time, which meant being up with her a large part of the night. Why did her child need so little sleep?

Pulling the covers up to her chin, Louise wondered what time it was, but didn't care enough to look at the bedside clock. She did notice Eliot wasn't there. Was he taking care of their daughter so she could sleep in? If so, she didn't want to disappoint him by getting up.

"Good morning, Mommy," he said in a cheerful voice that was the opposite of her mood. "Look who's here."

He laid a contented Cynthia beside her on the pillow, and Louise forgot her rough night. Her heart swelled with love for the beautiful new person God had put into her care, and she was a little ashamed of herself for being grouchy about her interrupted sleep.

"Isn't she the most adorable baby you've ever seen?" she murmured, touching her daughter's soft cheek with one finger.

"Let me think," Eliot teased. "My second cousin Annie's third baby was pretty spectacular, but she was born with the hair of a baby monkey."

"You're terrible!" Louise sat up and cradled Cynthia, taking care to keep her swaddled in her blanket.

"I hated to wake you," he said, "but the dean asked if I could stop by his office this morning. He has some questions about the class schedule for next semester."

"You're supposed to be on winter break," Louise protested. "And it's Saturday. Couldn't he just ask you on the phone?"

"Apparently not," Eliot said. "But I probably won't be gone long. Actually, I have a few things to ask him. I'll enjoy the break more if everything is settled for the next term."

"I thought we could spend the day catching up on jobs that need to be done." She knew it wasn't her husband's fault he had to go to the campus, but she could see her time for working on the stocking evaporating.

"Tell you what. When I get home, I'll take the laundry to the Laundromat. I hate to have you down in that dank basement when it's so cold."

"I'd really appreciate that," she said. "It would take forever for things to dry down there, and Cynthia's things would be stiff and musty smelling."

"I'll put Cynthia in her bed so you can get dressed," he said, lifting her from her mother's arms. "Don't worry. I'll get back as soon as I can.

Louise wasn't optimistic. The dean was a nice man, but he loved the sound of his own voice. Eliot could be tied up in his office for hours. It didn't seem fair when this was the first day of his Christmas vacation, but then, nothing was going quite as planned this year. She certainly hadn't expected to be called upon to direct the concert on such short notice, even though it was an honor to be asked.

After she had a quick breakfast of oatmeal and tomato juice— the only kind she had in the house—Louise felt reenergized. There was no reason why she couldn't do a little work on the stocking while her husband was gone. In fact, it might be better to work while he was out of the apartment.

Things didn't go quite as she'd intended. Her sister Jane phoned, and while it was always a pleasure to talk to family, Louise had a hard time getting back on track after their conversation. Then a young boy came to the door offering to shovel the front walk. She hated to turn down a child, but the scant snow covering hardly warranted the price he was asking. Besides, Eliot liked to clear it himself because his job didn't give him much chance for exercise.

"The best made plans of mice and men may oft times go astray," she said, quoting one of her father's favorite phrases.

Cynthia seemed to sense her mother's eagerness to sew and thwarted it by being especially colicky. When Eliot did finally get home, she made a late lunch for the two of them and realized a trip to the market was imperative.

Her frustration peaked when she got two calls from choir members only minutes apart.

"I am dreadfully sorry," Amanda, one of the older women in the group, said. "My daughter and son-in-law are both down with this nasty flu that's going around. I have to go to Cleveland and help them out with their three children. I'm almost sure I won't be back for the concert. I'll probably just spend Christmas with them—if I'm fortunate enough not to catch their bug."

"I'm terrible sorry," Louise said, assuring her it was the right thing to do.

Amanda had a nice voice, but she wasn't one of the strongest vocalists. Louise hated to lose any member of the choir, but others in her section would be able to compensate for her absence.

The second call worried her more. With Cynthia on her shoulder vocalizing in her own unique way, Louise struggled to hear what the soloist with a cough was saying.

"The doctor says I can't possibly sing Christmas Eve," she croaked in a barely audible voice. "I'm sorry to let you down."

After offering sympathy to the soloist, Louise was ready to panic. She had to find someone who was qualified to take over her part, but she didn't know the choir members well enough to be sure of a replacement. Her only recourse was to call the director who was sidelined and get her suggestion. She was a lovely woman who couldn't have been more helpful, but she was also a talker. It took some spectacular howls from Cynthia to cut short the conversation. Then, of course, she had to make another phone call to line up the replacement.

"Want me to do the grocery shopping?" Eliot offered when she finally got off the phone.

"No, I know just what we need. It will be faster for me to go."

"Well, the streets are a little slick. Drive carefully," he said.

Did he think she was going to drag race through staid Philadelphia neighborhoods? Louise left in something of a huff, although she was the first to admit it was fatigue and frustration, not real anger.

She'd forgotten how long the checkout lines could be on Saturday, especially since the weather report was calling for snow.

After wheeling her own cart out to the car because the boys who were hired to do it were overwhelmed, she managed to get home with five heavy sacks to carry up the slick front steps of the brownstone.

In the apartment, Eliot was just about done feeding Cynthia, and he wanted to hurry to the Laundromat. The machines were apt to be busy, so he took a book along to pass the time while he waited.

Louise envied him the quiet hour or two spent reading, but the streets were getting slippery, and she had to change the baby and put away the groceries, a job she preferred to do herself because her husband could be a little too creative about where to put things.

At least she had a free evening to work on the stocking, she thought as they sat down to a TV dinner of Salisbury steak, corn, and mashed potatoes that evening. It was a poor substitute for home cooking, but all she had time to prepare.

"I have a wonderful idea," Eliot said as he finished and laid down his fork.

"Oh?" She was battling waves of fatigue, but was hopeful she'd revive when she started work on the stocking.

"Let's start a tradition of our own: an evening to relax and enjoy the Christmas carols we both love."

"This evening?"

Her heart sank. How could she refuse to spend time with her husband after he'd done the laundry, hauled it up to the apartment, and put most of it away himself? He was worn out from end-of-semester responsibilities, not to mention being short on sleep. He deserved some quiet recreation with his wife.

But she was exhausted too, and all day she'd looked forward to working on the stocking.

"Maybe you could play records while I sew. That way we can both enjoy the music, and I'll get some work done on the stocking."

His silence said more than words could.

"I won't work late, but next week is going to be terribly busy," she said. "We have rehearsals every evening, and it's almost impossible to work during the day. There are so many interruptions."

"Louise," he said in a solemn voice, "please be reasonable. You're exhausted, and you've already ruined fabric because you're too rushed to take pains with your sewing. Let's make popcorn and hot chocolate and enjoy each other's company for a change— at least as long as our daughter lets us."

She sighed, not wanting to argue but disappointed by his attitude. Even though he was right that Cynthia would not know when her special stocking was made, he still didn't understand how important it was to follow her mother's traditions. Nothing she could say was going to sway him.

"All right, I'll make popcorn," she said, trying to conceal her disappointment. "I guess we deserve it after a TV dinner."

Her hope was that Eliot would fall asleep on the couch, and she could get some sewing done before she woke him up to go to bed.

Instead, Louise found it impossible to keep her eyes open. She snuggled beside him and let the wondrous carols wash over her, but she fell asleep with her head on his shoulder long before she finished her bowl of popcorn.

The following week disappeared in a haze of fatigue as Louise held rehearsals, wrapped gifts, addressed Christmas cards, mailed packages to her sisters and father, and finished Christmas baking. Cynthia seemed to have her days and nights mixed up, although she rarely went more than a couple of hours without needing her mother's full attention. Eliot kept busy working on plans for the next semester, frequently going to his office on campus for a quieter space.

The stocking lay on the table, untouched but not forgotten. Louise kept telling herself that she had plenty of time to work on it, but other responsibilities always seemed to keep her from it. How on earth did her mother manage to get everything ready for Christmas and still give her daughters all the attention they needed?

Christmas Eve came quickly. In the past week, Louise had been busy tending to Cynthia and running rehearsal every night. She hadn't had time to work on the stocking, and she was frustrated, but the day before Christmas was one of the most beautiful days she'd seen in Philadelphia. The grime of the city and the roofs of brownstones on her street were covered with glittering white, and the gently falling snow didn't keep people from coming out on the holiest of nights. Louise was gratified by the turnout for the concert, especially since it meant congregating in spite of the very real fear of the Asian flu. As she watched the crowd fill the pews in the sanctuary, she prayed that the musical program would be inspirational as well as entertaining.

In the choir room, everyone was robed and ready, although Louise was a bit worried about the substitute soloist. Lucinda was a high school student recommended by the church choir director, even though she didn't sing regularly with the group. A petite, dark-haired girl with huge brown eyes, she was nervously wringing her hands as she waited to march in.

"You'll do just fine," Louise said, hoping to calm her.

"Sometimes my voice squeaks when I'm nervous," she confessed.

"You're probably not half as nervous as I am," Louise said with a light laugh. "Anyway, this is a very friendly audience. They don't expect perfection."

The choir sang beautifully in spite of several absent members, but the part of the program that would stay in Louise's memory forever was Lucinda's solo. She stepped forward and began "Oh, Holy Night," while everyone listened in silent rapture. Louise's eyes were teary as the familiar words reminded her of the birth of the Savior. Mary had been a young girl herself when she brought forth the Christ child, so who better to sing of that sacred event than a teenager?

Lucinda's voice didn't squeak. Quite the opposite. The words flowed from her. When she finished, Louise could see she was pale and shaken by her own performance, but it had been flawless.

After the congregation filed out, still awed by the beauty of the soloist, Louise hurriedly received congratulations and met her husband. She'd prevailed on Maxine to watch Cynthia, but she didn't want to take advantage of her by lingering at the church.

"It was wonderful," Eliot said, helping her with her coat. "You certainly brought out the best in the young girl."

"It wasn't me," Louise said thoughtfully. "The Lord inspired her."

When she remembered Lucinda's pre-concert fear, her performance did indeed seem like a miracle.

The two of them arrived home to a second miracle, albeit a tiny one.

"She's sleeping like an angel," Maxine said as she pulled on her boots to leave, "It was a lovely way to spend Christmas Eve."

Louise sent her home with a plate of cookies and many thanks, then turned her attention to the table with her portable sewing machine. Somehow the week had flown by with no time to finish Cynthia's stocking. She had presents wrapped to put in it, but the fabric was still lying there in pieces.

"At last I can get this sewn," she said, sitting down at the makeshift table.

"You're not going to sew now, are you?" he asked.

Eliot's disappointment pricked her conscience, but how else could she give her baby a Christmas stocking?

"It won't take long. I have everything planned out. All I have to do is stitch it up and put on the finishing touches." This wasn't strictly true, since she intended to appliqué Cynthia's name on one side and finish it off with rickrack she'd found in her mother's tin workbox.

"There's no way I can talk you out of it, is there?" her husband asked with resignation.

"No, but you could make tea. We can celebrate the evening with a Christmas cookie."

He grumbled, but put together a little snack of cheese and crackers to go with the cookies. Louise had been too nervous to eat before the concert, so she was more than grateful for the gesture.

"I'll just nibble while I work," she said. "This will go fast."

"It's after ten. Can't you come to bed now and finish tomorrow?" he asked in a dispirited voice.

"No, I'll do it now, and tomorrow we can have the whole day to celebrate Christmas."

He picked up a library book he wanted to finish before it was overdue, but soon he gave up and went to bed.

Although she kept telling herself she could easily finish before Cynthia's midnight feeding, she started having trouble with the quilted material almost immediately. It was too thick to flow easily under the foot of the machine, and several times she had to stop and start over after putting in only a few inches of stitching.

"I hate this machine," she said, wondering if hand sewing would be more efficient even if it would take longer.

She gave it a try, but forcing the needle through the thick layers hurt her fingers, and she never had mastered the use of a thimble. How could she be so proficient on the piano and all thumbs when it came to sewing?

Most of her snack was sitting untouched on the edge of the table, and she took a few moments to eat a cheese square and a frosted cookie. But the cookie only reminded her of how wonderful Christmas was with her mother, and she returned to the machine, determined to sew the back and front of the stocking together.

The machine jammed almost immediately. She tried to inch the fabric out from under the foot, knowing if she pulled too hard it would rip. Tears rolled down her cheeks, and she couldn't hold back her sobbing.

"Are you all right?" Eliot asked, coming into the room in his robe.

"No, the machine won't sew."

"Come to bed, darling. You can finish tomorrow." He gently put his arms around her as she sat, and she was greatly tempted to give up on the stocking.

"I can't," she said miserably.

"I've never known you to be so stubborn," he said, obviously making an effort not to sound angry.

"Go back to bed." She just couldn't deal with an irate husband and a cranky sewing machine at the same time.

"No, not until I understand why you're driving yourself to finish the stocking when Cynthia won't know the difference. You could make it in July, and it wouldn't matter to her."

He pulled up a kitchen chair and sat down beside her.

"It's not just a stocking," Louise said, sniffling. "I want to be the kind of mother Alice and I had. I know how life was hard for her, but she always made Christmas wonderful for us."

"You see your mother as perfect and want to be like her," Eliot said thoughtfully.

"Yes, I want to walk in her footsteps." Louise swiped the back of her hand across her eyes. "She loved us so much and left us so soon. The least I can do is try to be like her for Cynthia."

Eliot leaned forward and took her hands in his. "Don't you know you're already an amazing mother? You're unique and special. When our daughter is old enough to realize how blessed she is to have you, it won't be because you've tried to do everything as perfectly as your mother did."

"You're just saying that to make me feel better about being a failure." Louise took a tissue from a nearly empty box on the table.

"No, I'm saying it because it's true." Eliot moved so he was across from her and looked directly into her eyes. "Look how hard you've worked on the stocking already. You're as devoted to your daughter as any mother can be. You don't need to make her a stocking to prove that."

Louise didn't say anything. She watched her husband, who was gazing at her with pure love on his face. Big wet tears were coursing down her cheeks.

"My darling Louise, there's something Cynthia needs more than a fancy Christmas stocking."

"And you're going to tell me what that is," she said, forcing a smile through her tears.

Eliot laughed and handed her another tissue. "Your daughter needs a mother who loves her enough to put aside this compulsion to be perfect. That would be a true gift for Cynthia—the ability to keep our priorities straight. She needs us to not aim for goals that interfere with the thing that matters most: love."

Louise hated to admit it, but she knew Eliot was right.

"Can I still finish the stocking, just to be done with it?" she asked with a broad grin. She wiped her eyes and stuffed the tissue in her pocket.

"*We'll* finish the stocking," he said, surprising her. "Let me take a look at the machine. I'm no mechanic, but maybe I can get it going again."

She was too surprised to protest.

"Here's the problem. The thread is all jammed up under here." He slid off the little metal plate below the needle and pulled out a tangle of bright red thread. "Now rethread it and see how it goes."

He sat by her side as she managed to make fairly straight lines of stitches. Their beloved daughter slept through the hum of the machine, and the fabric finally took the form of a big bright stocking. The rickrack and Cynthia's name could wait for another day, she decided, overwhelmed with gratitude as her husband stayed by her side.

"My mother didn't do everything perfectly," she admitted. "One Christmas, she didn't realize the holiday turkey was fully thawed. She overcooked it so much it was dry and stringy. Alice and I ended up snacking on popcorn and hot apple cider, and the turkey was cat food for quite a few days."

"Was your mother upset?" Eliot asked.

"Perhaps, but she never let us know. My father was a good sport too. I believe he convinced her to open a can of Spam to go with our sweet potatoes. Now that I think back, it was her attitude that made her such a good mother."

She held up the stocking, wondering why the toe looked so small. Her seams were uneven, giving it wavy sides, but it was still big enough to hold Cynthia's small gifts.

"It's beautiful," her loving husband said. "Where should we hang it?"

"Oh dear, I completely forgot about a loop at the top. It won't hang." All Louise could do was laugh.

"We'll lay it on the back of the couch and take a picture of Cynthia and the stocking. You'll see, someday it will be a beautiful memory," Eliot said.

Louise nodded.

"Our daughter's first Christmas will be memorable enough. She's blessed our life more than I can ever express." Louise's eyes were moist, but this time her tears were joyful.

"She's the most perfect gift of all," her husband murmured, leaning close and pressing a warm kiss on Louise's damp cheek.

Cynthia cried out so loudly, she startled both her parents. Louise laughed and hurried to pick her up, while Eliot took a bottle of formula from the refrigerator.

"Merry Christmas," he said, laughing while he warmed Cynthia's midnight snack.

"It is indeed a blessed Christmas," Louise said smiling down at the precious gift in her arms.

*D*addy was right, you know," Cynthia said, wiping a tear from the corner of her eye. "I love my stocking, and to me, it is perfect, and so are you. I'm sorry I was such a colicky baby, though."

"You were a perfect baby," Louise said. "Thankfully, the colic only lasted a few months, for your sake and mine."

"Yes, it's a good thing, or I would be suffering now, after stuffing myself with your delicious food, Aunt Jane." Cynthia patted her stomach and laughed.

"That was a fabulous breakfast," Alice said. "Eating the sweet bread and licking my fingers took me right back to my childhood."

"I'm glad you liked it, but you can thank Mother's recipe. I couldn't improve on that one." Jane grinned. "If I'd had her recipes when I worked at the Blue Fish Grille, I'd be a famous chef by now."

"That would be our loss. We couldn't run the inn without you," Alice said.

"We wouldn't have tried," Louise said.

"I thank the Lord you did," Ethel said. "I'm glad you girls want to keep the old traditions alive. It brings back such sweet memories, it's almost like having my dear Bob and Madeleine and Daniel with us. In spirit, anyway."

"I feel that way too," Alice said. "Jane, why don't you change while we all clean up from breakfast? We're all dressed for church."

"All right. I'll meet you in the living room so we can open our gifts." Jane put down her napkin and left the room.

Alice finished washing the dishes and left the others to dry and put them away. She took a cup of tea and went into the living room. The fire had died down, but the room was toasty warm. Since they'd be leaving for church in a while, she left it alone. She took a closer look at Cynthia's stocking. It did look well used, like a child's favorite blanket.

Glancing up, Alice noticed the old family nativity set on top of the mantel. The baby Jesus was in the manger. Had it been there earlier? One of their traditions, since they were children, was to place the baby in the manger after Father read the biblical story. They still observed that practice as a reminder of the reason for Christmas. One of her sisters had done it this year without her, which made her a little sad. She shrugged. At least they were all together. That's what was important.

Jane came down, dressed in an ankle-length flowing red and green skirt and a soft cotton poet blouse with a long paisley scarf draped artfully around her shoulders. Her hair was twisted up in a French knot in the back. Though she wore jeans most days, she loved vintage styles and had a flair for fashion.

"You look festive. Is that new?" Alice asked.

"Yes. I made it last week. Do you like it? I have a lot of left-over fabric. I could make you a skirt."

Alice laughed. "Nice try. But no thank you. You know I don't wear skirts if I can help it."

Jane smiled. "Yes, but it's fun once in awhile."

"If you say so. Say, Jane, did you put the baby Jesus figure in the manger?"

Jane glanced toward the mantel. "Not I. I wondered about that too. It was there when I came downstairs. If you didn't do it, perhaps Louise put it in after we went upstairs last night."

"What did I do?" Louise asked as she and Cynthia and Ethel came into the living room.

Alice and Jane turned toward their sister. "Did you put the baby Jesus figurine in the manger?" Alice asked.

"No." Louise's right eyebrow formed a peak as she looked from Alice to Jane. "I assumed Jane put it in, since she was the first one up this morning."

"It was there when I came downstairs. Neither of you put it in the manger?"

Both sisters shook their heads.

"Cynthia, did you put it in the manger?" Louise asked her daughter.

"Nope. I figured one of you did it this morning when you were reading the Bible story."

Jane turned to Ethel. "Did you put it in, Auntie?"

Ethel held up her hands. "I wouldn't do that. I know you girls always put it in the nativity after your father read from the Bible. It's a tradition."

"*Hmm.*" Alice rubbed her chin. "It seems we have a mystery."

"Well there's another mystery here," Jane said. "What is in those stockings? I say we find out." She walked to the fireplace and removed the stockings one at a time, handing each one to its owner.

Alice, Louise and Jane took their stockings and sat on the couch. Ethel and Cynthia sat in the chairs. Everyone looked at Louise.

Louise reached into her stocking. Cynthia giggled.

"What's funny?" Louise asked. "Is there a mouse trap in there or something that will jump out at me?"

"No. I was just thinking that you three remind me of the three monkeys on a log in one of the children's books I edited this year. The oldest one got to eat the first banana. Then they went in order of age, just as you three do every year at Christmas opening the stockings."

Ethel laughed out loud. "I never thought of monkeys, but you three are creatures of habit."

"*Humph.* As long as nothing is going to jump out or snap at me, I shall proceed," Louise said. She pulled out the ornament attached to the top of the stocking. "Oh! It's beautiful." She held up a white bisque snowy owl with gray markings. Every Christmas there was an ornament tied to the top of each stocking—something that had significance for the year. It was a tradition their mother had started when they were young. "I'll never forget seeing that owl in the field last winter. A line of cars had stopped to watch it swoop down on a hay field. Most of the snow was gone, so it must have spotted a rabbit or some large rodent. I wished I'd had a camera. I didn't find out until the next week what a rare sighting it was. It should have been up north by the Arctic Circle."

"It's such a special blessing to see something rare like that," Alice said.

Louise carefully set the three-inch-tall ornament on the coffee table, then dug through her stocking, finding a bookmark decorated with a tassel of beads, a satin drawer sachet, hand cream, a scented candle, candies and fruits and nuts.

"Your turn, Alice. What did you get?" Jane asked.

She reached in and pulled out her ornament. "Oh." She held up a shiny red glass covered-bridge ornament about four inches long. It had a snow-covered roof and icy blue water under the bridge. "It looks just like the Pine Grove Bridge I saw on the field trip with Vera's class last March. I had to treat scrapes and cuts on Charles Matthews' arm and hand when he tried climbing on the side of the bridge and fell."

"I remember," Louise said. "He missed two weeks of piano lessons."

It was Jane's turn. She reached into her stocking and pulled out the ornament. A smile lit her face. She held up a small silver square hanging on a red ribbon. Two white ermines were painted on the square. "I love it! Remember the ermine that hung out in the yard last winter? It kept trying to get into the net-covered balls of suet I put out for the birds. Its antics were so funny. It'd climb up and hang on the balls, spinning around while it tried to rip open the balls. It would finally succeed, so I put out suet balls with bits of raw bacon and other meats. I haven't seen him this year, but I got so much joy out of watching him. He visited every day while I worked in the kitchen."

Cynthia's ornament was a monkey with a wreath around its neck. "What a cute monkey. Just like the ones in my new series. Thank you, Santa."

Ethel had a red rhinestone-covered high-heeled shoe ornament. She loved red and fancy shoes and lots of bling. She held up the shoe and let out a dramatic sigh. "If only I could still wear heels this high."

The sisters rose and hung their new ornaments on the tree.

"There's the cone you made for me, Jane," Louise said, placing the new owl high on the tree near the other ornament.

"Yes, and there's the bicycle I got the year I learned to ride," Jane said.

"And the spatula you got the first year we opened the inn," Alice said. "And there's the little dog I got the year I helped organize the adopt-a-pet-for-Christmas drive for the animal shelter."

"I remember that year. I was afraid we would have to adopt them all," Louise said.

"Did I tell you how close I came to bringing several home with me?" Alice said. "It's by God's grace that didn't happen."

"God's grace and Louise putting her foot down." Jane laughed.

"I eventually came around," Louise said indignantly. "And it worked out quite well in the end, as I recall."

Alice's
Christmas Memory

*W*alking side by side in downtown Acorn Hill on Saturday morning with her best friend Vera, Alice found it hard to believe it was exactly two weeks until Christmas. The air was crisp but not cold, and she admired the early afternoon sunlight glittering off a diamond dusting of snow.

"I'm glad you suggested coming this way," Alice said as they slowed to look at a Christmas display of elves and reindeer.

"I thought it would be fun to peek in the shop windows," Vera said. "Besides, when we're done we can go to the Coffee Shop for a treat."

A Danish could undo all the benefit of their aerobic activity, but a cup of hot tea would hit the spot when they finished their walk.

"That's a good idea," Alice agreed. "Oh look." She pointed at the window of Parker Drugs as they walked past the pharmacy. The store somehow managed to retain its old-fashioned feel and still provide up-to-date service.

Vera paused beside her at the small storefront window, where a diorama showed a snowman 'soda jerk' serving up snow cones to snowmen, women, and children.

"That's so cute," Vera said.

Alice agreed. "I love the tiny dollop of whipped cream on the miniature sundae," she said.

"On the way home, we'll have to stop by the hardware store so you can see what Fred did for our Christmas display," Vera urged, sounding proud of her husband's efforts.

"Did he go all out?" Alice asked, following her friend down the sidewalk, where other residents of Acorn Hill were taking advantage of the pleasant day.

"You'll have to see for yourself," Vera said, flashing Alice an impish grin.

"Now you have me really curious," Alice said. "Let's head that way and forget about the Coffee Shop. I'll be too tempted by their sweet rolls anyway."

As they crossed the street, Vera looked back. "I think we're being followed."

"What?" Alice stopped and saw a dog hanging back by the pharmacy. "We don't see many strays in Acorn Hill. Maybe he's waiting for his master to get something in the store."

"Maybe," Vera said doubtfully. "Let's head toward the hardware store and see if he follows."

Alice looked back over her shoulder as they walked, a little surprised when the dog walked in their direction.

"Are your fifth graders excited about Christmas?" she asked to distract her friend. Vera was a teacher at the elementary school, and she was worked hard to make school fun as well as educational for her students.

"Are they! I don't know who's more eager for the break, them or me," Vera said with a sigh. "We won't accomplish much next week, since the kids know they have the week before Christmas off."

Alice quickened her pace as they neared Fred's store, but Vera paused a moment and had to hurry to catch up.

"I hope he's friendly," she said nervously, "because I think we've made a new friend."

Glancing back, Alice had to agree. The dog did seem to be keeping pace with them from a distance, although, unlike Vera, she never felt threatened by animals. In fact, they were the delight of her life, especially Wendell, their family cat who thought he was master of Grace Chapel Inn.

"Oh my!" Alice exclaimed, peering into the window of the hardware store. A wintry Christmas scene of miniature tractors and cars was laid out on folds of white fabric sprinkled with glitter to resemble snowflakes. A tiny train chugged its way around a track, flanked by toy houses, barns, and a perfectly shaped church with a white steeple. Small evergreens were 'planted' in the fake snow.

"Isn't it grand?" Vera asked, beaming at Alice.

"Oh yes," Alice agreed. "It's perfect. I didn't know your husband was this creative."

"His clerks did most of it. Fred was more than happy to take over stocking shelves and waiting on customers while they gussied up the place for Christmas."

Alice smiled. "I know Fred is compulsive about keeping things organized, but he's a good boss too if he let his employees do this enchanting window. Since we're close to the inn, would you like to come home with me for a tea break? Jane has been baking up a storm for Christmas. I'm sure there are some cookies she hasn't frozen."

"I'd love to," Vera said, "but I won't stay long. I have a long list of things to do today. Fortunately, I'll have a full week off before Christmas this year."

"I'm taking off the week before Christmas too," Alice said. "In exchange, I'll be working the following week, when some of the young nurses want to be home with their children. Now, let's go to—" Alice's words were cut off when something darted in her path.

"*Whoa!*" a startled Vera cried out as the dog tailing them raced up, then hovered a few steps away from them.

Alice didn't feel threatened, but she was curious. The dog was a she, and medium-sized, with a glossy tan coat and a scruff of white fur. She couldn't see any tags on the collar, and the canine appeared to be limping.

"C'mere girl," she crooned, holding her hand out, but the animal shied away.

"Poor thing," Vera clucked sympathetically. "She looks like somebody's pet."

Alice thought the same thing. Despite the absence of tags and the slight limp, the dog looked too well groomed and healthy to have been living on the street for very long. Bright brown eyes and perky ears gave her an inquisitive look.

"If only you could talk and tell us where you belong," Alice said to the dog. She was relieved to see the animal's bushy tail was still raised upright and wagging a bit, instead of cowering between her hind legs.

Vera knelt down beside her and cautiously stretched out her hand too, but the dog still backed away.

"We can't just leave her here," Alice said, and Vera nodded in agreement.

"What kind of dog do you think she is?" Vera asked.

Alice scrutinized the animal. "Seems like a spaniel mix, but I'm not sure what else. Look at that tail," she said, gesturing at the white-tipped still-wagging tail. "You're right about not leaving her here, and I know my sisters won't want me to bring her home to the inn. Would you mind skipping our tea break if we can coax her to come to us? We could take her to the Humane Society shelter between here and Potterston."

"That's no problem," Vera said, rummaging through her purse.

"Great," Alice sighed in relief. "Wendell wouldn't be very happy either if I brought a dog home. What are you looking for?"

In answer, Vera brought her hand out of the depths of her handbag. "Aha!" She brandished a well-worn package of beef jerky at Alice.

"Vera, you're a genius!" Alice said to her friend.

Shrugging modestly, Vera grinned. "I never know what ends up on the bottom of this handbag on any given day. I 'confiscated' this from one of my boys at recess and forgot to give it back. If I recall correctly, he was using it as a sword."

Alice took the proffered package from Vera and used her fingernail to slit it open. Kneeling down again, she held out her hand with the jerky in it. "Here puppy, here puppy," she crooned, purposely keeping her voice low and steady to coax the dog toward her.

Out of the corner of her eye, she watched as Vera unwound the old wool scarf she'd tied around her neck. Alice said a silent prayer of thanks for a good friend who'd anticipated her next need. If the dog did come to them, the scarf would serve as a perfect makeshift leash.

Slowly, the dog inched toward Alice, sniffing at the jerky in her hand. Sensing nothing dangerous, the canine took the treat, allowing Vera to carefully approach and loop the scarf around the collar.

"Good girl, what a good girl you are," Alice crooned, petting her as the dog quickly chomped down the meat stick.

"Well, we did it," Vera said, with a sigh of satisfaction.

"Thanks to you and your jerky," Alice said. "And I owe you a rain check on tea and cookies at the inn."

Vera chuckled and patted her waistline under her bulky coat. "I'll take you up on that for sure."

"Okay pup, let's get you out of the elements and we hope on your way to finding your home," Alice said. "Probably the first place your owners will check is the shelter."

"I'll get the keys from Fred, and we can take my car to the shelter," Vera offered. "He drove it to work this morning because his truck has been cranky about starting. "We have a couple of old blankets in the trunk."

Soon Alice was settled beside the dog on the backseat of the Humbert vehicle while Vera expertly steered them onto the road to Potterston.

At the shelter, Alice smiled at a small Christmas tree in a corner of the reception area. It was decorated with rawhide dog bones and fuzzy cat toys. They were quickly greeted by a tall young woman with a dark ponytail and a name tag identifying her as a volunteer named Sandy.

"May I help you?" Sandy asked, looking at the dog slinking close to Alice's legs, perhaps skittish because of the many strange scents or the faint sound of barking.

"Yes," Alice said, petting the pup reassuringly. "My name is Alice Howard, and this is my friend, Vera Humbert. We were out for a walk in Acorn Hill and found this stray. She doesn't have tags, but she looks too well fed and nicely groomed not to be somebody's pet. We thought maybe someone called you to report a missing dog."

"We haven't received any calls yet," the young volunteer said, "but we can certainly try to find the dog's owners. It's possible she has a chip with tracking info embedded in her."

"She certainly is a beautiful animal," Vera said. "Someone must miss her."

"I wish we could figure out what kind of mix she is," Alice said.

Sandy studied the dog thoughtfully for a minute. "She definitely has some spaniel in her."

"We thought that too," Alice said.

"Actually," Sandy said, peering over the counter to get a closer look, "she looks like she has some husky in her too."

"Husky!" Alice said. "We didn't see that, but now that you point it out, her tail and ears are obvious clues."

"You know," Vera said, "I've heard it's very trendy for dogs to have fancy mixed-breed names like labradoodle and schnoodles. . ."

"And if no one claims this one, maybe you can adopt her out as a 'spusky'—a spaniel husky," Alice said as all three of them laughed.

Sandy suddenly looked very serious.

"Is something wrong?" Alice asked.

"Well, all kidding aside, anything that helps get animals adopted is a good idea. It's very difficult to find homes for all the animals at the shelter, especially this time of year. Would you like to see our residents while I take 'Spusky' to our quarantine room? All new arrivals spend a short time set aside from the others."

Alice knew herself too well. It was a bad idea to look at all the sad-eyed creatures, since she couldn't take them home herself, but she still said yes. Handing over Spusky's makeshift leash, she and Vera followed Sandy through a door with an arrow that said 'Dog Kennels' on it.

First the young woman unlatched the door to the quarantine area and coaxed Spusky to go inside. Alice was surprised the stray went so easily, but the poor dear was probably exhausted from wandering. There was no way to know how far or long she'd roamed.

"I'll give her food and water as soon as you leave," Sandy said. "And I'll let our supervisor know right away that we have a new 'guest' so we can get her information online. Hopefully, someone will be worried and claim her soon. The rest of our guests are down here."

As they followed her, Sandy explained that there were always more males than females at the shelter. "And small dogs get adopted much quicker than the big ones, as I'm sure you can imagine."

They entered a room lined with large cages. At the end of the row, Alice saw a gorgeous Shetland sheepdog, tail upright and wagging.

"What a beautiful dog," she exclaimed. "I can't imagine anyone not wanting him."

"Isn't he sweet?" Sandy said. "That little sheltie was brought in by his in-town owners because he was just too energetic for their tiny yard and small children. Such a shame." She shook her head in dismay. "I'd take him home in a heartbeat if I had room. But I suppose my three cats would be highly displeased."

"What happens to all these animals at Christmastime?" Alice asked.

"It's just another day for shelter animals," Sandy answered. "The day is divided between staff and volunteers like me, so no one has to work a full shift. It's a sad day, though. Hardly anyone wants to adopt a shelter dog or cat to give as a Christmas present," she said. "Generally speaking, there aren't many winter placements."

"Oh, that is sad," Alice agreed, the slow germ of an idea forming in her mind.

"Would you like to see our kitties?" Sandy asked.

"Maybe not today, thank you." Alice was already so sad about the dogs, she was sure she'd break out in tears if she saw homeless cats penned up and unwanted.

Sandy led the way back to the reception area. "Ladies, thank you so much for bringing this dog in. We'll do our best to locate her owners."

"If you do find out whom she belongs to, would you please let me know?" Alice asked, requesting a pen and paper to leave her number. "I'll worry until I know she's home."

"Certainly. I know just how you feel. I love volunteering here on my days off, but sometimes I'm really sad about our homeless waifs."

As they left the shelter, Alice shivered. The day had grown much colder, and a brisk wind whipped around the corner of the shelter. But it wasn't the weather that troubled her. She felt heavyhearted about all the animals that wouldn't have a home at Christmastime.

Wendell rubbed against Alice's leg, an unusual bid for attention from the independent feline.

"You can tell I've been to the animal shelter, can't you?" Alice asked as she scooped him up. "I wonder how you'd like a playmate. Maybe a nice Shetland sheepdog."

Wendell yawned, showing his sharp little teeth, and Alice could imagine his indignation if she brought home a new pet.

When she put him down, he swished off with his tail held high.

"Nearly time for dinner," Jane said, sticking her head into the library where Alice had been brooding about the plight of the shelter's inmates.

"Wonderful! I forgot to eat lunch, and I'm famished," Alice said.

When she joined her sisters in the kitchen, she was surprised to see Aunt Ethel wasn't there. She'd been invited to join them for one of her favorite meals. When she asked about her, Louise explained that she was entertaining a friend for dinner in the carriage house. Their aunt rarely cooked for others, so Alice was surprised by the news.

"I think she gets lonesome for people her own age," Jane explained. "A woman she knew when she was still on the farm is passing through Acorn Hill. I invited Ethel to bring her here, but I think she wanted time alone with her to talk over old times. So I sent a chicken potpie and some yeast rolls for their dinner. That's what we're having too, so there was plenty."

"I hadn't thought about it, but I imagine Aunt Ethel does get lonesome at times," Alice said after the blessing. "Sometimes we get too busy to give her much companionship. Maybe she needs a pet to talk to."

"Whatever gave you that idea?" Louise asked, daintily breaking the crust on her portion of potpie.

"I guess all the homeless dogs and cats at the shelter got to me," Alice explained. "There must be lots of people in Acorn Hill who would enjoy a pet. In fact, a big house like ours could easily accommodate one more."

"Oh dear," Louise said, laying her fork down. "I know what a softie you are. You're not thinking of bringing home a stray, are you?"

"I hate the idea of ten dogs and half a dozen cats spending Christmas in cages," Alice said a bit defensively.

"We're running a bed-and-breakfast, not a home for stray animals," Louise said, sounding unusually testy.

"I don't suppose one more cat would bother our guests," Jane said, giving tentative support to Alice.

"You're forgetting about my Christmas concert a week from Thursday," Louise said in a distressed voice. "I can't have the inn overrun with animals when I have a friend from the National Piano Guild coming. She only visits relatives in Potterston on rare occasions. My best students have been practicing for weeks, and so have I."

"I wasn't thinking of bringing all of them here," Alice said. "Maybe just the sheltie and a couple of kittens."

"Oh dear," Louise said. "You're talking about a potential disaster."

"After our current guests leave, we don't have any scheduled until after Christmas. We wouldn't have to worry about anyone being allergic."

"Imagine what a couple of strange cats could do to the furniture. You don't even know if any of the animals at the shelter are housebroken."

"I wouldn't let them in the parlor," Alice said a bit indignantly.

"When did we ever keep Wendell from going wherever he likes?" Louise nodded as the cat strolled into the kitchen to investigate his feeding dish.

"Fine. I won't bring any of them here," Alice reluctantly agreed, a bit surprised by her older sister's vehement objection. It wasn't at all like Louise to be so out of sorts with either her or Jane.

Louise was as fond of Wendell as she and Jane were, but she probably did have a point. A new pet required a lot of attention. Even though Alice was taking vacation time the week before Christmas, it would be a busy time. But she couldn't get into the Christmas spirit knowing lost and abandoned animals would be spending the holiday season penned up.

Her work at the hospital kept her busier than usual, as she was filling in for a nurse who was taking vacation time. Alice liked the morning shift, even though a number of patients with seasonal illnesses kept the urgent care staff hopping. Still, her thoughts kept coming back to the sad-eyed animals at the shelter.

After work Tuesday afternoon, she decided there wasn't any harm in calling the shelter to find out whether Spusky's people had claimed her. If they had, it would be one fewer forlorn pet to worry about.

Fortunately, Sandy answered the phone, so Alice didn't have to explain her interest in the lost dog.

"Did you find Spusky's owners?" she asked.

"Happily, they found us," Sandy said. "They were in the process of moving to Acorn Hill when Blue—that's her name—wandered off and couldn't find her new home. They were frantic until they learned she's here at the shelter."

"That's such good news," Alice said. "I hope Vera and I didn't make their job harder by bringing her there."

"Just the opposite. They thought she'd been left behind at their old home. They did their own moving, and things were really hectic. Their worst fear was that she'd wandered off and been hit by a car."

"Then I guess they were really relieved," Alice said.

"They want to thank you, but I didn't know whether to give them your name," Sandy said. "They're picking up their dog at around five this afternoon. Maybe you'd like to come meet them."

"I'd love to if you think it's all right," Alice quickly agreed.

"They sound like lovely people on the phone. I'm sure you're welcome to come say good-bye to Spusky-Blue," Sandy said enthusiastically.

When Alice walked into the shelter, Sandy wasn't anywhere in sight, but a young couple in blue jeans and heavy winter jackets stood waiting with two little girls who looked to be around three and six years old.

"Are you Spusky-Blue's owners?" Alice asked.

"Yes, the shelter volunteer has gone to get her now. We're the Nielsens, Tom and Ramona," the man said. "This is Kasey and her sister Reese. Are you the lady who found her?"

"My friend and I did. I hope I did the right thing bringing her here."

"You did a wonderful thing!" Mrs. Nielsen said. "Blue had a fenced yard at our last home. She has no street smarts whatsoever. We were scared silly she might have been hit by a car."

"Blue!" the younger child shrieked when Sandy brought in the dog. She ran and hugged her, joined by her sister, who was just as happy to see their pet.

"As you can see, Blue is one of the family," Mr. Nielsen said. "Again, we can't thank you enough for getting her off the streets. Our first project this spring is to install a fence around our new back yard."

Alice watched with Sandy as the family left with Spusky— it was hard to think of the dog as Blue. She was happy for the Nielsen family but sad about all the other dogs and cats who weren't as fortunate.

"If I could have one wish for Christmas, it would be to see all the animals in the shelter spend the holiday with people who would love and care for them," Alice said.

"Yes, I know how you feel," Sandy said. "It's the hardest part of working here, knowing some animals will never find homes."

"I wonder. . ." Alice was thinking furiously, trying to find a solution to the problem. "No, it wouldn't work."

"What wouldn't work?" Sandy asked.

"I read a story once, a long time ago. It was about an orphanage that convinced people in the community to take an orphan home for the holidays so every child could experience Christmas with a family. It had a happy ending. Some of the orphans got adopted by their host families."

"Was it a true story?" Sandy asked.

"I can't remember," Alice said laughing. "But I do remember thinking how kind people can be. I wonder if the idea would work with animals."

"Are you suggesting temporary homes for our cats and dogs over the holidays?" Sandy sounded skeptical, and Alice didn't blame her.

"The more I think about it, the more I like the idea. The schools will be closed next week. The shelter could lend out pets to keep children occupied in the days before Christmas with no obligation to keep them—the animals, not the kids." Alice knew it was a wild idea, but not an impossible one.

"A week is plenty of time to get attached to a pet," Sandy said, "but the shelter doesn't have the personnel to carry out a big project like that on such short notice."

"Would there be any objections?" Alice asked.

"The director is out of town, but I could send her an e-mail and ask," Sandy offered. "In fact, I'll do it right now. Would you like to visit our guests while I do?"

"I'd love to!" Alice said. "I haven't been able to get the Shetland sheepdog out of my mind. He's a beautiful dog and shouldn't be penned up."

Sandy let her wander back to the dog kennels on her own. A chorus of barks greeted her as she walked past the cages, looking at all the beautiful animals in the wire enclosures. She stooped in front of the sheltie, fervently wishing she could take him home and keep him. Louise was right, though. Grace Chapel Inn was a business, and they had their hands full without trying to shelter stray animals.

"We have to find a good home for you," Alice said, stooping and reaching her hand through an opening to let the dog sniff her fingers.

Stifling tears, she went back to learn the results of Sandy's e-mail to her boss.

"She thinks it's a wonderful idea," Sandy said, "but the shelter doesn't have the resources—the people or funds—to undertake such a big project."

"Would she object if I try on my own?" Alice impulsively asked.

"Not at all!" Sandy excitedly assured her. "She's one-hundred percent behind any idea that will find homes for our animals. If even one dog or cat is adopted after Christmas, it would be wonderful."

"I have friends who love cats," Alice said. "I'm sure I'll find people who love dogs. I know almost everyone in Acorn Hill, not to mention the staff at the hospital here. I'm sure I can persuade people to take all your animals."

"I can't imagine a better Christmas present for everyone involved in the shelter," Sandy said. "Is there anything I can do to help?"

"I would love to show pictures to potential hosts. Is there any way I can get a photo of each dog and cat? I'll have copies run off after work tomorrow."

"You won't need to. We have a flyer for every animal available for adoption. The flyers have descriptions and as much history as we know. Maybe you've seen some on the grocery store bulletin board."

"Yes, I have, although I didn't pay much attention at the time."

"All the animals we have for adoption have had their shots and are in good health. That's an important point," Sandy noted. "I'll run off copies for you now if you have time to wait for them."

"Gladly," Alice said.

While Sandy printed out a generous number of sheets for each animal, Alice tried to make a mental list of people who might consider taking a pet for the holidays. When she got home, she would begin by enlisting helpers, since she couldn't possibly talk to every prospect herself. Vera might be willing to make an announcement to her class, and it wouldn't be hard to spread the word at the hospital. Jane might know a few people, but she'd better not bother Louise when she was so focused on her concert.

When Sandy handed over an impressive stack of flyers, Alice thanked her profusely. She wasn't going to let the forlorn animals dampen her love of the Savior's birthday, not when there was something she could do about them.

Now her first step was to tell her sisters about the project. She drove home with her head full of ideas.

At the hospital Wednesday, Alice intended to talk up her idea of taking home a pet for the holidays, but she was much too busy to do more than mention it to a few friends. Not only that, her mind was full of other things she had to do before Christmas.

For one thing, she'd forgotten to pick up a book she'd ordered as a gift for her special friend, Mark Graves, the head vet at the Philadelphia Zoo. He was hard to shop for, but her friend Viola Reed at Nine Lives had ordered a beautifully illustrated book about the endangered species of Africa.

Now that she thought of it, she could pick up the book after work and tell the shop's owner about her pets-for-Christmas project. No one in Acorn Hill loved cats more than Viola, which made her a good prospect to take at least one from the shelter.

Viola was busy with a customer when Alice walked into her shop, so she browsed until the owner was free.

"You're going to love this book," Viola said enthusiastically when she and Alice were the only ones in the shop. "It's even nicer than it looked online."

"I hope Mark doesn't already have it," Alice said.

"Unlikely, since it's hot off the presses," Viola assured her, laying it on the counter for Alice to inspect. "But if he does have it, I'll be happy to exchange it. In fact, I may order more copies. I have several customers who are interested in preserving endangered species."

"Speaking of endangered animals," Alice said, seizing the moment to bring up her project, "the animal shelter has a full house for Christmas. I'm trying to help place some in homes. My idea is to have people take a pet for the holidays with no obliga-tion to keep it."

"Sort of a trial adoption," Viola said thoughtfully. "I imagine most people would get attached and want to keep their guest pet."

"That's what I'm hoping. I know you have quite a few cats. . . ."

"Nine at last count," Viola said with a small laugh, flicking back the long gold and green silk scarf around her neck.

"Is there any chance you could take one more?" Alice asked.

"I'd absolutely love to, but there's a problem. Gatsby—you know I name all my cats after literary figures—has been out of sorts lately. It's made him hard to live with, and I'm afraid a new cat would stress him too much."

"Is he the big black and white?" Alice asked.

"Yes, seventeen pounds of feline fury when he's aroused. The others avoid him, but I'm afraid a newcomer might become a target."

"I shouldn't have asked you," Alice said. "You already have a house full of cats to take care of."

"Nonsense! You don't know how tempted I am to adopt one of the shelter's strays, but it's not possible right now. Maybe I can help you in some other way."

"That would be wonderful! I have a stack of flyers in my car. Maybe you could post a few in your store window and talk up my project. I need all the help I can get."

"It shouldn't be too hard to get people to take an animal for the holidays," Viola said. "It's a great way to discover whether a pet is right for a family."

"I hope you're correct," Alice said, mentally counting the ten days until Christmas. It didn't seem like much time to place ten dogs and six cats, but she was determined to give it her best effort.

"My helper can watch the shop for a couple of hours tomorrow afternoon," Viola said. "Why don't we go out together when you're through with work? I'll make a list of people who might be willing to take a pet on a trial basis, and we can make some house calls."

"That's a wonderful idea! I can't tell you how much I'd appreciate your help," Alice said as she completed the transaction for the book.

"It will be fun, but let's go by car instead of traipsing all over town. My feet have had it after a long day in the store."

"Good idea," Alice agreed, glad she wouldn't have to worry about Viola tripping over one of the long skirts she habitually wore. "I'll come by the store as soon as I can tomorrow afternoon."

Buoyed by Viola's enthusiasm, Alice went home with her mind full of possible prospects.

Unfortunately, her friend June Carter, owner of the Coffee Shop, was out of town visiting family in Philadelphia for the holidays. She headed a feline rescue group and no doubt would be willing to help. Alice thought of calling her for advice, but decided against it. June worked exceedingly hard, dividing her time between her business and rescue efforts. She deserved a change of scene without taking on Alice's cause.

She was going to call Mark that evening. His support always meant a lot to her, and he loved animals as much as she did, although his favorites tended to be big, dangerous carnivores.

In the kitchen of Grace Chapel Inn, Jane was putting the finishing touches on a batch of cutout Christmas cookies.

"You just missed sprinkling colored sugar on the frosted ones," Jane said. "Did you have to work overtime?"

"No," Alice said, eager to tell about her activities since leaving the hospital.

"It's an ambitious plan," Jane said thoughtfully after hearing what Alice had done so far. "I've tried to think of ways I can help, but I really don't know many people who might be receptive to taking a pet over the holidays. I can imagine what an untrained dog or cat could do to pretty packages and decorated trees."

Alice sighed. Jane was right, of course, but pets didn't have to be given the run of the house. All they really needed was food, water, and human compassion.

"I'm sorry we can't take in a cat or two," Jane said, "but I'm afraid Louise is right. This isn't a good time to introduce a newcomer into the family. If it were summer. . ."

"I understand," Alice said. "But surely there are people in town who've been thinking of getting a pet but haven't done anything about it yet."

At dinner, Louise was sympathetic about the pet project but equally determined not to introduce a new animal to life at Grace Chapel Inn.

"You're gone all day, and I'm much too busy getting ready for the Christmas concert here," she said in her usual practical way. "The responsibility would fall on Jane, and she already has more than enough to do."

Alice had to agree, but she still hoped to place all the pets at the shelter in homes before Christmas. After helping Jane clean up after dinner, she was eager to call Mark. He would understand what she was trying to do and might have some helpful suggestions.

He answered on the second ring, and the warmth in his voice made Alice glad she'd called.

"What's going on in Acorn Hill?" he asked.

After explaining her goal of placing all the shelter animals for the holiday, there was a long silence on his end of the line.

"You don't think it's a good idea, do you?" she asked in a disappointed voice.

"I think it's a wonderful idea and typical of the way you care for God's creatures," he said. "I was just trying to come up with ways to help you."

"Your encouragement has helped me already," Alice said. "I know this isn't the best time of year to ask people to temporarily adopt a pet, but it was heartbreaking to see all those lonely animals in cages."

"I understand," Mark said. "Even zoos are trying to get away from the practice of caging their exhibits. Whenever possible animals should be allowed to live in a setting as close to their natural environment as possible. I do have one suggestion."

"Tell me," Alice urged.

"Why don't you talk to your local vet? He would know about any pets that have passed away lately. Their owners might want to replace them."

"That's a great idea," Alice said. "I know how sad I'd be if something happened to Wendell. A new kitty might console me. I'll call Dr. Blair tomorrow and see if we can talk to him after his office hours. Viola Reed agreed to make some calls with me."

After they chatted about other things for nearly half an hour, Alice hung up, glad she'd gone to Mark for encouragement. She had ten days until Christmas, and she was going to place all the dogs and cats if it took every free moment she had.

True to her word, Viola was ready and waiting when Alice got back to Acorn Hill after her shift at the hospital.

"I have a few prospects for you," Viola said as she entered the passenger side of Alice's car. "I wrote down their addresses. Where do you want to start?"

The bookstore owner carefully adjusted her long woolen skirt so it wouldn't pick up dampness from her dainty, high-heeled boots. Light snow had been falling all day, turning to slush as the temperature rose. It wasn't a pleasant day for house-to-house canvassing, and Alice was afraid her friend would soon be shivering in her forest-green waist-length jacket. Viola would fit in well in one of the Victorian novels she loved, but her outfit wasn't very practical for December in Pennsylvania. In fact, much as Alice appreciated her company, she was afraid her friend might fall in the impractical footgear.

Fortunately, she had an alternative plan.

"I called Dr. Blair. He's expecting us any minute now. Mark gave me the idea of talking to the vet first."

"Good plan!" Viola said enthusiastically. "Maybe he'll take a few himself. He's so good with my cats. Even Gatsby seems to like him."

When they got to the vet's parking lot, Alice came around the front of the car and gave Viola her arm. Much as she appreciated help on her project, she didn't want to be responsible for her friend falling. Although they were close to the same age, Viola was considerably heavier and not as steady on her feet.

Still wearing his white lab coat, Dr. Casey Blair greeted them in his empty waiting room. He led them to his small office opposite the examining room.

"Thank you for waiting for us," Alice said.

"No problem," he said, pushing up his wire-framed glasses. "I have a surgery patient who needs watching for a while yet. In fact, there's so much hustle and bustle at my house, I'm in no hurry to go home. My in-laws are coming this weekend for the holiday, and my wife's mother is allergic to cat and dog dander. Kristin is doing all she can to make the house safe for her mother."

"That's a worry at the inn when we have a guest who's allergic," Alice said. "We haven't had much success getting rid of

Wendell's dander, but we try to keep him confined to areas where guests don't need to go."

"Well, I'm afraid Kristin's mother will have to rely on her allergy medicine, but my wife is cleaning from top to bottom," Dr. Blair said. "Now what can I do for you?"

"I've taken it upon myself—with help from Viola—to place all the cats and dogs at the animal shelter in homes for the holidays," Alice explained.

"Temporary adoptions?" The vet pursed his lips and looked skeptical. "I wish you luck, but this isn't a good time to introduce a pet into a household."

"I know," Alice said. "But I can't get those poor caged animals out of my mind."

"It's worth a try, isn't it?" Viola asked.

"Of course, and I'd be the first to take at least one cat if my mother-in-law wasn't coming. Is there any other way I can help you?"

"We were hoping to get names of pet owners who suffered recent loses," Viola said. "I know a new kitty is always a comfort to me when one of my cats passes on."

"Oh dear," Dr. Craig said sounding distressed. "There's nothing I'd like better than to help you that way, but professional ethics won't let me reveal the names of people in my practice."

"Yes, I certainly understand medical ethics," Alice said, trying to sound cheerful about it. "There's no reason why the rules shouldn't apply to a veterinary practice."

"Well, I wish you the best of luck. It's great of you ladies to take on a project like this. I know the shelter doesn't have the personnel to do it."

Walking back to the car, Alice tried not to be downhearted. Mark only worked in a zoo setting, so he couldn't know how conscientious their local vet was about privacy. Nonetheless, his idea had been worth a try. She still thought people who'd lost a pet would be ideal candidates to adopt a shelter animal.

"What next?" Viola asked as she buckled the seat belt.

"Let's make one more call. Whom do you think is most likely to say yes among those on your list?" Alice asked.

"Maybe a family with children old enough to care for a pet themselves," Viola suggested. "My neighbors certainly qualify, but perhaps I should speak to them alone. It would seem more casual, and I could give them time to think it over. If we both show up on their doorstep, I'm afraid they'll immediately say no."

"Is there anyone on your list we should see together?" Alice asked, trying to rally her own enthusiasm.

"I'm nearly out of my favorite blend of tea," Viola said. "Why don't we stop at Time for Tea. Wilhelm Wood is a lovely man. Maybe he'd like to bring a cat home for Christmas."

Alice doubted the owner of the shop would be interested in a pet since he traveled extensively, but she parked near his store and again helped Viola navigate the slush that was beginning to freeze solid on the street and sidewalks.

The shop was empty except for a young clerk, but Alice did enjoy inhaling the exotic fragrance.

"Is Mr. Wood in town?" Viola asked after selecting several boxes of tea.

"No, I'm sorry. He's spending the holiday season in Iceland. Something about wanting to see a hotel carved out of ice," the girl said. "Will there be anything else?"

While Viola paid for her purchases, Alice decided to buy a box of chamomile tea. At the moment she couldn't imagine anything more pleasant than a long soak in a hot tub and a fragrant cup of tea.

"You wouldn't like to adopt a cat or dog for the holidays, would you?" Viola asked the clerk.

"Ah, no," the startled young woman said. "I'm afraid my birds would be a tempting lunch for anything with fur."

Viola left the shop in high spirits, but Alice couldn't share her enthusiasm. Obviously they needed a better system for finding potential people to adopt pets.

"Shall we try the bakery?" Viola asked. "I might pick up some of their delicious poppy-seed rolls for dinner."

"If you like," Alice agreed.

As she expected, the clerk at the Good Apple bakery had no interest in a pet, but Viola got a bag of nice rolls. She was happy to let her friend shop, but it wasn't getting them any closer to success with the shelter animals.

"It's nearly dinnertime," Alice said, giving up for the day and driving Viola to her shop to get her car.

Snow was coming down harder, and the leaden sky above matched Alice's mood. It was going to be very hard to persuade people to take a temporary pet when her own sister didn't see merit in the plan. Jane hadn't objected, but she was obviously snowed under with decorating the inn and baking cookies, including some for Louise's concert.

"Did you have any luck placing shelter animals?" Louise asked over a simple meal of baked fish and roasted vegetables.

"Afraid not," Alice admitted.

"If it were summer—" her older sister started to say.

"Yes," Alice agreed. "It is going to be hard to convince people at this time of year. I wish I could show animal lovers how dismal it is for friendly pups and abandoned kitties to be caged up at the shelter for Christmas."

"I don't think the animals know it's Christmas," Jane commented mildly.

At that moment Wendell pranced into the kitchen with his tail held high. In spite of her discouragement, Alice had to smile at his antics. He was king of the inn, no doubt about that. It would require a lot of patience and work to introduce a rival into his domain, but she liked to believe the inn was large enough for family, guests, and a visitor from the shelter. Jane adored cats and wouldn't be hard to convince, but she couldn't blame Louise for not wanting a new pet when she was working so hard on her concert.

"What are you going to do next?" Jane asked.

"I can't do much until I begin my vacation next week," Alice conceded. "But I fervently believe the Lord looks down with favor on those who care for the least of his creatures. I'm not going to give up."

"Somehow I didn't think you would," Louise said with a broad smile while Jane nodded agreement.

⌒

"The results are disappointing so far," Alice said as she and Vera conferred with Viola on Saturday, the first day of Vera's winter vacation.

Although the store had just opened, several people were already browsing the well-stocked shelves. It was easy to see that Viola wasn't going to have much time to think about the shelter pets one week before Christmas.

"How many are left?" Viola asked between helping customers locate what they wanted.

"All but one," Alice said. "I did persuade a nurse on my shift to take a cat for her aunt. She's going to stop by the shelter and pick the one she wants."

"So that's one down, fifteen to go, if you count cats and dogs," Viola said with a worried frown. "I wish I could help you more, but as you see, this is a really busy time for me."

"I'm glad to see it," Vera said. "Books make wonderful gifts. In fact, I may come back later to see if I can finish my Christmas shopping here."

"You've already been a big help," Alice said, smiling at the cat flyers tacked on the framed pictures of Viola's favorite classic authors. "The black cat does look a little like Poe if you look at it just right."

Both of her friends chuckled, then Viola had to scurry away to help a potential buyer.

"Let's finish our walk," Vera suggested. "Maybe the crisp, cold air will inspire us."

"More likely it will freeze our toes and fingers," Alice said, not in her usual cheerful mood. She picked up her canvas bag with the extra supply of flyers, but obviously Viola didn't need more yet.

"One of the clerks at Fred's store is tempted to take a cat," Vera said as they walked, "but her husband isn't keen on the idea. We'll see what happens there."

"Oh dear," Alice said. "I knew placing pets would be a hard sell, but I didn't expect it to be impossible. I prayed about it, but I'm still fresh out of good ideas."

Walking beside Vera in the downtown area, Alice suddenly came to a stop.

"Isn't that a wonderful display?" Vera asked, following Alice's gaze to a store window decorated with angel figurines.

"That's what the shelter animals need," Alice said, excited by a new idea. "Guardian angels."

Vera gave her a puzzled look but didn't say anything.

"And I know just where to find them," Alice said, feeling more optimistic than she had in days.

"Guardian angels for dogs and cats? I know you love animals, but—"

"My ANGELs!" Alice exclaimed.

"Do you mean the middle-school girls in your church group?" Vera asked. "Yes, I can see where they might be helpful if their parents approve."

"I've had wonderful support from parents in the past," Alice said. "I'll ask their permission before I get the girls too involved, but this could be the answer."

"Yes, children seem to have a natural affinity for animals, especially cute cuddly ones like our kitties and pups," Vera said. "Are you meeting with the ANGELs this week?"

"Not officially, although most of them are signed up to help with Christmas festivities at Grace Chapel. As soon as I get home," she said, resuming their walk, "I'm going to make some phone calls."

The rest of the walk went by quickly, and Alice hardly noticed her numb toes and stinging fingers. She was heated up by enthusiasm and could barely wait to enroll her ANGELs in the project.

When she and Vera parted near the inn, Alice decided to talk to the Matthews family in person if they were home. They lived fairly close to the inn, and she was too fired up to mind a few extra blocks of walking. Their daughter Sissy was a sweet, helpful girl who regularly attended ANGELs' activities. She might even be willing to call a few of the group for Alice. Making ten calls could take quite a while, and Alice would feel a bit guilty if she didn't help Jane for at least part of the day. They still had guests booked through Wednesday.

When she got to the Matthews' cozy clapboard house with a picket fence surrounding their lot, Alice couldn't help but see the yard as a good place for a dog to play. Whether they were willing to take a pet on a trial basis was another thing, but at least it was worth a try.

Sissy's brother answered the doorbell and invited her into the front room. He was around ten, with reddish-blond hair and a sprinkling of freckles that made him look mischievous, but he couldn't have been more polite. It was a good beginning, though Alice really needed to talk to his parents.

"Are Sissy and your parents home?" she asked when he looked inclined to leave her by herself.

"Yeah, Mom is." He gave a loud yell, and Mrs. Matthews quickly came into the room.

"Oh, Miss Howard, Sissy is out back taking out the trash. I'll call her."

"Just a minute," Alice quickly said. "There's something I should ask you first."

After briefly explaining her goal of placing shelter animals for Christmas, Alice held her breath for a reaction.

"That's a lovely idea," Sissy's mother said.

"I can show you some photos with information about them," Alice said, glad she had a supply with her.

Sissy came into the room, her cheeks bright red from the winter chill, and dropped her vibrant pink jacket on the nearest chair so she could look at the picture with her mother.

"We've been wanting a dog for ages," Sissy said with a beseeching look at her mother."

"It's a big decision," Mrs. Matthews said. "I would only adopt one if both you and Charles promised to be responsible for it."

Her son crowded close to go through the pictures, and the two siblings began picking favorites.

"That's the nice thing about this idea," Alice pointed out. "You're under no obligation to keep the animal after Christmas. Think of it as a temporary adoption. There has to be a good fit between people and their pet, so there's no pressure to keep one if it doesn't work out."

"I have to admit I like the sound of that," Mrs. Matthews said.

"Look at this one, Mom," Sissy said, holding up a flyer for her mother to see.

"It's a pointer-setter mix," Alice said, "so we've decided to call him 'Pointsetter' in honor of the Christmas plant."

"I love him already," Sissy said, echoed by her brother.

"Well, if it's only for a week or so, I guess we could have a trial visit if both of you promise to do all the work yourselves," their mother said with a loving glance at her children.

Charles whooped with pleasure, and Sissy gave her mother a big thank-you hug.

"Do we pick him up at the shelter?" Mrs. Matthews asked.

"No, since you've made your choice already, I'll be happy to get him for you this afternoon. Keep this flyer so you know his background. You'll see that he's had all his shots, and the shelter guarantees he's in good health. They send home a bag with dog food samples and additional information with every pet."

"I can hardly wait!" Sissy said. "I'm going to call Emily and Linda and tell them about this great project."

"That would be wonderful," Alice said. "Be sure to tell them to have their parents call me if they have any questions. And, of course, it would be great to have the names of anyone besides the ANGELs who might be interested in a pet."

As she hurried back to the inn, Alice went over the list of names she needed to call. Briana was out of town for the holidays, but that still left a number of ANGELs who might be willing to help, even if they couldn't adopt a pet themselves.

When she got home and went into the kitchen, she didn't need to tell Jane how happy she was.

"I haven't seen you smile like that for a week," her sister said. "Did you have a nice walk?"

"Great! I actually placed one of the big dogs with the Matthews family. And I'm going to contact all my ANGELs for help. Who better to know families who might accept a temporary adoption than middle-school girls?" Alice gratefully took a cup of hot tea from Jane, but she could hardly wait to start making phone calls.

"Do you need me to do anything right now?" Alice asked.

"No, go take care of your abandoned pets," Jane said with a knowing laugh. "You're not going to enjoy Christmas until each and every one has a home for the holidays—even if it is temporary."

"I have a good feeling about that," Alice said. "I don't think many people will be able to return a pet once it settles into their homes."

Her luck held as she phoned the rest of her ANGELs in the library of the inn. Her father's favorite room encouraged her to be bold in asking for parents' cooperation, although her project proved to be an easy sell. Not all ANGELs agreed to take a pet, some needing time for the family to think about it. But all the girls who were spending the holidays at home offered to look for possible leads.

Best of all, Lisa Masur had been delighted at the prospect of owning a cat. She called Alice back an hour or so later and let her mother talk.

"We've decided to try two cats if you have them," Mrs. Masur said. "Both of my girls want one of their own, so to keep peace in the family, we'll take a kitty for each. How can I get them?"

"You can go to the shelter yourself, or I'll pick them up for you."

"I don't know much about cats," the mother admitted. "But I trust your judgment. Would you mind selecting two that would be compatible with each other for the trial visit?"

"I'd love to!" Alice agreed. "I'll consult with the person working at the shelter to get the best pair. I'm going there this afternoon, so I'll bring them to your house before dinner. And just so you know, all animals have their shots and come with an information pack and food samples."

Although she couldn't wait to get to the shelter, Alice called ahead to give them advance notice and ask the best time to come. Fortunately, Sandy was working, so there was no need to explain the situation.

"That's wonderful!" the volunteer said. "Your friend from the hospital picked up one cat, so that's half of our kitties with a place to go for Christmas. You did well to place the 'Pointsetter' too. He's young yet, and a little rambunctious, but he's a beautiful animal. It's a shame big dogs aren't adopted more often."

Alice set off in midafternoon with high hopes. Fortunately, the shelter lent out carriers, so she would be able to transport two cats and a dog by herself, although she hadn't quite worked out the logistics.

'Pointsetter,' who came to the shelter without a name, was so excitable he was hard to coax into the carrier, but the felines, an adult tiger cat and a black-and-white kitten, were cuddly and easy to handle. Alice explained how she was enlisting the help of her ANGELs, and Sandy was as excited as she was.

"If you can place even half the animals, it would be great," the volunteer said.

"I'm hoping to find temporary homes for all of them," Alice said optimistically.

Her first stop was the Matthews' home, where Sissy and Charles were watching at the front window for her arrival. The carrier was too heavy to lift by herself, so she attached a shelter leash to the dog's collar and led him to his home for Christmas.

The whole Matthews family was in the front room to greet their canine guest. Sissy's father was as excited as the children, getting down on the floor to romp a bit with the half-grown dog.

"He's a good mix," he said enthusiastically. "I don't think he'll be hard to train once he settles in here."

Alice quietly took leave of the family, greatly pleased by their reception of the 'Pointsetter.' If Lisa and the Masur family liked the cats this much, she'd done a good day's work.

As it happened, she needn't have worried.

"She's beautiful," Lisa said, quickly choosing the younger cat as her special pet.

Fortunately, her sister was just as happy with the tiger cat, planning what toys to give it for Christmas.

"This is really a good project of yours," Mrs. Masur said. "We've been thinking of adopting cats to replace the one we lost a few years ago, but we kept putting it off. You've made it easy."

"I hope you love them both," Alice said, stroking the little cat's head before she left. "And if you know anyone else who might be interested, there are still three cats and nine dogs who would love to be in a real home for Christmas."

Her happy glow lasted until she got home. As wonderful as it was to see three animals placed in good homes, she still had twelve who weren't so fortunate. Would it be possible to find people willing to give them a trial visit? With only one week until Christmas, Alice prayed for a small miracle. Her heart still ached for the caged animals in the shelter, especially the Shetland sheepdog, who deserved a much better life.

"I talked to Fred, and he agreed we should take the little Pekinese that may be part Lhasa apso," Vera said on the phone.

"Wonderful!" Alice said. "I'll cross that one off my list."

"How many do you have left to place?" her friend asked.

"Three cats and eight dogs, not counting the one you're taking," Alice said, consulting her list, although she had the number in her head.

"Oh dear, that's quite a few, isn't it?" Vera asked. "I wish I could be more help, but Fred needs me at the hardware store. He rarely asks me to help out, but his new line of miniature toys has been selling like mad."

"Of course, family comes first," Alice said, wondering what Jane had for her to do this Monday. She could hardly refuse to help get the inn into top shape for Louise's concert, but she hoped there would be some free time to work on her project.

The call ended with Vera promising to pick up her canine guest at the shelter, saving Alice a trip. Now she needed to check with Jane to see what remained to be done.

Her younger sister was up to her elbows in flour, baking cookies to be served at church after the Christmas Eve service.

"If you don't mind, I'd really appreciate it if you'd take my books back to the library. I took out a stack of them to look for new cookie recipes, and they're due today," Jane said.

"I'll be happy to." In fact, Alice wanted to ask the librarian, Nia Komonos, whether she would take one of the animals. The prospect of placing eleven more animals in homes for Christmas was daunting, even with the help of her ANGELs.

The library was relatively quiet, with only a few elderly men reading newspapers and a family with three young children looking for books. Alice deposited Jane's books on the return counter and saw Nia helping a patron at one of the library's public computers. She waited a few minutes until she was free.

"Alice, good to see you," the slender, dark-haired young librarian said. "Are you taking this week off?"

"Yes, but I'm busy with a new project. Vera and I are trying to place all the pets at the animal shelter in homes for Christmas."

"That's a lot to find homes for," Nia said thoughtfully.

"I know you're living alone right now," Alice said. "Have you ever considered trying out a dog? We're not asking people to adopt them right away."

"I imagine it would be hard to return a pet to the shelter after getting used to it," Nia said smiling.

"Truth to tell, we're hoping that's the case. But we still have quite a few to place. Is there any possibility. . ."

"I'd love to have a dog," the younger woman said, "but I work too many hours. It wouldn't be fair to keep one cooped up all day—even if my landlord agreed. Do you have any cats? When I lived at home, we always had several. I've missed having one of my own."

After quickly digging the flyers out of her purse, Alice told her about the three still available for a temporary adoption.

"They're all adorable!" Nia said with enthusiasm. "I imagine an older cat would do better left alone all day. Do you know why this one was left at the shelter?"

Alice pointed at a picture of a Persian with lovely light hair. "Her owner had to go into a nursing home, and no one in the family was willing to take responsibility for her pet. I imagine the former owner would be greatly relieved to know her 'Candy' found a good home."

"You've convinced me," Nia said. "Candy will be my house guest for the holidays. If we're compatible, we'll be roommates."

"Wonderful! Would you like me to pick her up for you?" Alice asked.

"No, I'm going to Potterston this afternoon for some Christmas shopping. I can easily stop at the shelter on the way home. I'm glad you came to the library today." Nia grinned broadly. "I'll have to be very stern with myself so I don't end up taking home two."

After profusely thanking her, Alice hurried home, hoping to hear good news from one of her ANGELs.

"Any messages?" she asked Louise, who was busy working on the inn's accounting in their father's former office.

"None that I know of. How many shelter animals have you placed?"

"Not enough," Alice admitted. "There are still two cats and eight dogs to place."

"I'm sorry we can't take any here," Louise said with compassion. "If it weren't for my concert—"

"I understand," Alice said. "Can you think of anyone who might be interested?"

Louise pursed her lips thoughtfully. "Florence doesn't have a pet. She would be hard to convince though. I think Ronald is fond of animals, but she's pretty particular about her house."

"Still, the Simpsons have a big house," Alice mused. "They wouldn't need to let a pet into the Victorian parlor. I guess it wouldn't hurt to ask them."

"You could try Aunt Ethel too," Louise suggested. "She really doesn't have enough to occupy her time."

"I know she's home because she just popped in to talk to Jane," Louise said. "Why don't you ask her now?"

Alice wasn't optimistic, but she made her way to the carriage house where her father's half-sister had lived since becoming a widow and selling the family farm.

"Aunt Ethel," she said when her slightly plump, red-haired aunt came to the door.

"Oh, Alice, I'm so happy to see you!"

This meant she was bored and wanted to have a long conversation, something Alice really didn't have time for. But she was too kind to rush off when her aunt was in a talkative mood.

A half hour of visiting passed slowly. Her aunt tried to keep abreast of all the town's gossip, but at last she ran out of 'news' to tell Alice.

"What are you doing with your week off?" the older woman asked.

"Trying to give the dogs and cats at the shelter a place to go for Christmas," she said.

"What do you mean?" Ethel asked, her pale blue eyes puzzled.

Alice explained, answering a dozen questions and finally bringing out the flyers.

"Have you ever though of getting a cat?" she asked.

"Oh my goodness, no! At the farm we always kept the cats in the barn. I really wouldn't want one in my home," she said a bit indignantly. "Not that Wendell isn't a suitable pet since all of you like him."

"What about a dog?" Alice asked without much hope.

"Dogs can be so much trouble." Ethel patted her short-cropped hair, a sign that she was thinking hard. "But they can be cute."

"The nice thing about the Christmas project is it's only a trial. You could send your visiting pet back to the shelter after the holidays if the two of you weren't compatible."

"I'll do it," Ethel said, surprising Alice. "Of course, I can't drive to the shelter."

"I'll be happy to bring your visitor here—and take him back if that's what you decide," Alice said.

"Splendid," Ethel said. "Now let me look at those flyers one more time before I pick."

Her aunt seemed quite taken with a small mixed breed with big eyes and floppy ears. There wasn't much history on the handout, but his people had moved and weren't able to keep a pet in their new apartment. Alice hoped for the best, suspecting her aunt would adore her new, lively visitor.

Encouraged by her aunt's enthusiasm, Alice decided to try Florence Simpson, a self-proclaimed pillar of Grace Chapel. She wasn't always the easiest person to get along with, but she had a good heart and a great deal of energy for a woman in her seventies.

Before she lost her nerve, Alice decided to pay a surprise call on Florence. She went on foot to her house because Vera wasn't going to have time to walk that day.

Even though Alice had come on a Monday without calling ahead, Florence was carefully made up, with her dark brown hair worn in stiff beauty-parlor curls. It was always a little startling to look into her broad face because she plucked her eyebrows to an ultrathin line and penciled them heavily.

"Alice, what brings you here today? Aren't you working at the hospital? I should imagine there are lots of sick people now that winter is here." Florence gestured for her to come in out of the cold, indicating a chair in the foyer where she could leave her coat.

"I just put the kettle on," Florence said. "Ronald brought me a lovely assortment of imported tea just last week. Can I fix a cup for you? You'd probably like the jasmine, although it isn't a favorite of mine."

After two cups with Aunt Ethel, Alice felt positively soggy, but she graciously accepted the tea, allowing Florence to be a good hostess and still get rid of a flavor she didn't like.

It took nearly twenty minutes for Florence to give her a complete rundown of all her important responsibilities during the holiday season. Most people, including Alice, appreciated all she did for the church and the community, but it came at the price of patience. Florence wasn't one to hide her light under a bushel.

At last, after two cups of rather bitter tea, Alice had a chance to talk about her shelter project.

"You mean, you're putting strange animals into people's homes? I know you mean well, Alice, but is that safe? They could have diseases."

"Every pet that leaves the shelter is healthy and has had all its shots. They all come with an informational packet and sample products." Alice had the feeling she was going through every detail for no reason, but she had her stubborn side too.

"It's been a long time since we've had a pet here. They're so hard on the carpets, not to mention the furniture, if they're not well trained. Are you sure they're all housebroken? How can you tell if they come from the shelter?"

"We can only take the word of former owners," Alice said patiently.

"My family always had purebred bulldogs when I was growing up," Florence mused. "My parents wouldn't have a dog without papers."

"I'm afraid the shelter doesn't have any registered dogs, but mixed breeds have a good reputation as family pets. In fact, they have a terrier-bulldog mix. Let me show you the picture."

"Oh, isn't he a cutie," Florence said, much to Alice's surprise. "What does it say about his history?"

She read the description and studied the picture on the flyer for so long that Alice got antsy.

"Poor thing. Imagine being abandoned outside a roller rink in Potterston. He must have been terrified when he ended up in a cage."

"Yes, most of the animals at the shelter have sad stories, although none they have now appear to have been abused," Alice said, at a loss to tell Florence more about the dog that had caught her eye.

"You did say this is just a trial adoption?" Florence asked.

"Absolutely. It's a way to get the poor things out of cages for the holidays. If the visit doesn't go well, people are welcome to return them. I'll even come and pick up any animal who's rejected." She hadn't planned to make that offer, but she wanted to encourage Florence as much as possible.

"I'll do it!" Florence said. "I won't promise to keep him for the whole holiday season, but if your terrier-bulldog mix is as well trained as he is adorable, we just might add a member to the family. Of course, Ronald would have to agree."

Her husband was known to never disagree with Florence, so Alice's hope rose. Was it possible one of the most difficult women she knew was enthusiastic about taking a shelter dog?

"Well, I'm glad you thought of me," Florence said, sounding unusually humble. "There's nothing like a little four-footed friend to bring Christmas cheer into a house."

Alice was dumbfounded, but managed to thank Florence several times before leaving her house. Outside, she thanked the Lord for this temporary adoption and prayed it boded well for all the shelter animals. Now she just had to find hosts for two more cats and six dogs, one of them the Shetland sheepdog who'd captured Alice's heart. Would this beautiful animal languish in a cage for Christmas? She fervently hoped not!

~

"You had a phone call," Jane said Tuesday morning when Alice got back from a brisk but chilly walk with Vera. "Mark said to call him back."

"I'm surprised he's calling so early. This was the only time Vera could spare to walk, but I certainly wasn't expecting to hear from him." Alice rubbed her hands together to warm them and gratefully accepted a cup of tea from her sister.

"You won't know why until you call him back," Jane said in a practical voice that made Alice smile.

"I'll call from the library," she said, carrying the welcome hot beverage with her.

Mark's voice always gave her a lift, and today was no exception.

"What I really need to know is whether you still have dogs to place," he said after they exchanged pleasantries.

"Unfortunately, six dogs still need a home for Christmas. And to make it worse, four of them are big males, not what most people want as house pets."

"Well, I can help you out. I know two families who live in rural areas. They especially want security dogs that will watch over the children as they play outside. Naturally they have to be good-natured pets. If you have any that might work out for them, I can drive there today and take them back."

"That would be wonderful!" Alice said.

"I only have today off, but it would give me a chance to see you before Christmas."

"We can have our own little mini-Christmas," Alice said enthusiastically. "And you can go to the shelter with me to see if any of the dogs would suit your families."

"I can leave in minutes," he said. "I should reach the inn around lunch time."

"I'll alert Jane," she said with a light laugh, knowing full well Mark didn't expect a home-cooked meal from her.

After she hung up, Alice hurried to find her sister.

"Mark is coming for lunch," she announced. "He wants to take two dogs back with him."

Jane's enthusiasm took the form of meal planning.

"I was going to open a can of soup, but if Mark will be here, I can make homemade broccoli cheese soup. I know he likes it, and I have some fresh rye bread for grilled sandwiches. Fortunately, there are plenty of cookies in the freezer. I'll make up a plate to send home with him."

"He's coming to pick out dogs," Alice said with a laugh.

"Just an excuse to see you," her sister said with an impish grin.

The rest of the morning went slowly as Alice kept a wary eye on the weather. The hilly Pennsylvania highways could be treacherous in a snowstorm, but sunny skies were predicted for the rest of the day in spite of the low temperatures.

One thing she had to do was wrap Mark's Christmas gifts. Besides the book, she'd purchased a beautiful blue cashmere pullover that would look wonderful with his charcoal hair and beard. She still marveled they'd reconnected after so many years. When she was in college, she couldn't bring herself to marry a man who didn't profess the Christian faith, but Mark had since embraced it. Their relationship was far more substantial than it had been when she was an undergraduate.

He arrived without incident a little earlier than she'd expected, but she'd changed into her best navy slacks and a practically new soft pink sweater.

"Good to see you," he said, hugging her before shrugging out of the navy peacoat that was his favorite winter garb.

"I'm really excited to take you to the shelter," she said, "but first Jane has a nice lunch for you."

Mark praised Jane's cooking and inquired about Louise.

"She's at a pupil's house," Alice said, explaining the concert she was holding at the inn. "She'll be playing herself, as well as featuring her best students."

"I'm sorry I can't be here for it," Mark said. "But someone has to stay at the zoo, and I let most of my assistants have the holiday off. One has a new fiancée, and others have young children."

"And you're a very kind boss," Alice said, standing when the meal was over. "Shall we go to the shelter now?"

"Yes, I'm curious about these animals you're trying to place in homes."

Another, different attendant, was on duty at the shelter, but Alice's project was well-known to everyone who worked there. The young man was delighted to meet the head vet from the Philadelphia Zoo and showed them both every courtesy.

"It's great to see some empty cages, thanks to you," he said to Alice. "I'll bring leashes if you want to get better acquainted with any of the dogs."

"Let's see what you have here," Mark said, putting the somewhat nervous attendant at ease. "I have people interested in two large good-natured dogs."

"Oh, you'll want to meet Champ, our boxer," Anthony said. "I'd take him home myself, but my apartment isn't much bigger than his cage."

"How does he happen to be here?" Mark asked.

"He was a runaway. A farmer put him in his barn and called us. I'm afraid he'd been abused, but it didn't make him aggressive. In fact, he's a pussycat when it comes to interacting with people and other dogs. It's just unfortunate he looks fiercer than he is, so he hasn't been adopted yet."

Mark stooped when Champ came out of his pen and tolerated an enthusiastic face licking.

"I think Champ will be leaving with me," he said, directing a warm smile at Alice.

"We have only five dogs left, thanks to Miss Howard," Anthony said. "Here's our Shetland sheepdog."

Alice knelt and let her favorite pooch lick her fingers.

"He's pretty hyper," Mark correctly observed. "Shelties are working dogs. He should live on a farm where he can run off some of that energy."

Although she was disappointed because Mark wasn't taking her favorite, Alice certainly understood his reluctance to place him with young children. He was a handful in the best of times and did belong on a farm.

Using his experience as a vet, Mark carefully observed the rest of the dogs and settled on a big tan male who could only be described as a mutt. What the canine lacked in looks, he more than made up for in friendliness, which was the main criterion for putting him in a family with children.

Mark had his own disinfected carriers borrowed from the zoo and leashes he'd bought for the purpose, but he gladly accepted the shelter's information packages and free samples for the host families.

"If either doesn't work out, I'll take him to a shelter closer to home," he assured the shelter worker. "But I'm optimistic."

After the shelter visit, Alice knew Mark had to leave. It was a long drive, and he couldn't be away from the zoo any longer than necessary. She gave him his gifts, which he wanted to open on Christmas, and a bagged dinner of thick ham and cheese sandwiches, carrot sticks, and cookies prepared by Jane.

"So you won't have to stop for supper," Jane explained before leaving the two of them alone to say good-bye.

Mark took a small package out of his coat pocket and handed it to Alice.

"Merry Christmas, Alice. This goes under the Christmas tree," he said, hugging her good-bye.

"Just seeing you is gift enough. I can't tell you how grateful I am to have two lovely dogs going back with you."

"I'm hopeful both will be permanently adopted," he said. "They're going to good families."

"I never doubted it."

Much as Alice hated to see him drive away after such a short visit, her heart was singing with happiness for the two dogs in his van. Now she only had four dogs and two cats to place, and she had the rest of the week to do it.

She threw herself into chores around the inn, eager to help Jane after taking most of the day off. Louise didn't want a single speck of dust to distract from her upcoming concert. The parlor was large, and she'd arranged to borrow chairs from Grace Chapel to accommodate the number of people she'd invited.

"Jane said Mark took two dogs back to Philadelphia," Louise said, coming upon Alice as she was standing on a ladder to dust a chandelier in the foyer.

Before answering, Alice climbed down. "Yes, but there are still six animals to place. We have such a big house. . ."

"Yes, but we also have guests through tomorrow evening and an important concert scheduled for Thursday. A good review from my friend could mean scholarships for some of my pupils. And I don't need to tell you I'm nervous about playing myself. This is the first time I've done something quite like this."

"I feel uncomfortable urging other people to take an animal when I'm not doing my part. I really can't see how a temporary adoption would affect your concert." The more Alice thought about it, the more upset she became.

"I just don't want to deal with a new animal this week," Louise said insistently.

"This is my home too." Alice couldn't believe she'd said these words, but it was true. She shouldn't need Louise's permission to bring a guest to the inn, especially if the guest was a lovable pet.

"Please, let's not talk about this now!" Louise said. "I need to practice."

Alice noticed Jane standing a short way from them. Her younger sister looked shocked. Alice and Louise rarely disagreed, and when they did, they talked things over rationally. As far as Alice could see, Louise was being more selfish than reasonable, taking over the whole inn for her concert. It wasn't as if an animal would be barking along with the music.

"She's nervous about the concert," Jane said when Louise went into the parlor to practice and shut the door after her.

"And I'm upset to leave some poor, unwanted animals in the shelter. It's not as if I want to bring all six that are left here."

"I just made tea. Would you like some?" Jane asked.

This time Jane's tea couldn't help. Alice excused herself and went to the library, a room where she felt especially close to her beloved father. Surrounded by the books he adored, she felt more peaceful, but still disappointed in her older sister.

The Victorian house that was now Grace Chapel Inn had been her home far longer than it had been Louise's. She was the one who'd lived with their father until his death, and, in fact, she'd never lived anyplace else that seemed like home. She didn't want to be juvenile, but it hurt that her sister was so set against bringing a poor, abandoned animal home for the holidays.

Turning to the Lord as she always did in times of stress, Alice silently prayed for a resolution to her problem, one that wouldn't fracture her relationship with Louise. She was sure God loved animals and would smile on her efforts, but her mood still remained bleak.

"The week went so fast," Alice said as she helped Jane put fancy appetizers on pretty plates. "Here it is, Thursday already. My days off have flown by."

"I'm glad Louise's concert is tonight," Jane said matter-of-factly. "She's been a bundle of nerves."

"I'm afraid I haven't been as sympathetic as I should have been," Alice said. "I've been so worried about my shelter animals, but the ANGELS have come through with flying colors. We're down to two, a big old tabby and the sheltie."

It would be so easy to bring both of them to the inn, but Alice didn't want to push Louise again. Things had been tense enough the past few days, and she didn't want to make them any worse.

"Isn't Louise's friend from the National Piano Guild a lovely lady?" Jane said as she put the plates in the fridge. "I can see why Louise wanted the concert to be perfect for her."

"Which I'm sure it will be," Alice commented.

She was glad they'd gotten acquainted with Jeanetta Sagers. Because the weather was uncertain, she'd been their guest the previous evening, and wouldn't go to her relatives' house in Potterston until Friday morning. Although Alice hadn't known what to expect, she was delighted to meet Jeanetta. She was a lovely, gracious person, perhaps the same age as Louise, but with an unlined face and soft white hair she wore in a bun.

As happy as she was to lend a hand to get ready for the concert, Alice couldn't help but feel downhearted. She'd fallen in love with the rambunctious sheltie, and now he would be the only dog in the shelter for Christmas. He wouldn't even have the fun of barking at other canines or romping in the exercise run with them. She felt lonely just thinking about him, not to mention the big sluggish cat that hadn't won the approval of anyone.

When it came time for the concert, Alice helped out by greeting the performers, their parents, and other invited guests at the door. It wasn't a huge crowd, but every borrowed chair in the parlor was taken when they were all there.

After taking a seat by the guest of honor, Alice settled back to enjoy the musical program that began with student pieces. Louise had chosen wisely, and her pupils performed to her credit, playing traditional Christmas songs by noted composers.

But it was Louise's own performance, the climax of the evening, that brought tears to Alice's eyes. Louise was nothing short of magnificent, and all the guests rose to give her a standing ovation at the end.

"It was lovely, all of it," Jeanetta said. "I feel so privileged to be here." She hurried up to the piano to congratulate Louise, and Alice's heart swelled with pride at her sister's accomplishment. And suddenly, Alice realized that Louise had been right. She could see why her sister had been worried about having an animal around. A new pet was unpredictable, and it would have been a terrible shame if something had gone wrong and ruined the concert. As horrible as she felt about the sheltie, she knew she'd made the right decision.

The next morning, after their guest left, Alice finally had time alone with Louise.

"I'm sorry I made an issue about bringing pets here," she said. "I shouldn't have bothered you when you were working so hard on the concert."

"I'm the one who should apologize for being cross. It was so gratifying to play for my friends, I realized you deserve the same sense of accomplishment. Your project at the shelter is just as important to you as a successful concert was to me." She gave Alice a big hug, an unusually demonstrative gesture from her reserved sister. "Later this morning you and I are going to the shelter. It's not too late for me to help you reach your goal."

Surprised by Louise's offer, Alice didn't know what to say.

"We'll have a guest for Christmas after all," her sister said in a firm, no nonsense voice.

"There's only one dog left, the Shetland sheepdog," Alice said. "He's young and so frisky no one wanted to take a chance on him. But there is a pudgy older cat who wouldn't be much trouble as long as we keep it separate from Wendell."

"We'll decide when we get to the shelter," Louise said.

The shelter was unusually quiet when they got there. A bored-looking young man was in charge, but he brightened when Louise told him they were there to select an animal for Christmas.

"We've never had so few to choose from, thanks to you, Miss Howard," he said nodding at Alice.

It did seem a bit eerie to walk through the almost deserted dog area, but the sheltie greeted them with a chorus of barks, jumping up on the wire fencing that confined him.

"Isn't he beautiful?" Alice said, letting him lick her fingers.

"Put him in a carrier, please," Louise said to the shelter worker. "Now I believe you have a cat too."

Dumbfounded by her sister's change of heart, Alice was overcome by happiness. Not only was her project a complete success, she could bond with the sheltie until he wore out his welcome at the inn—which she was afraid would be fairly soon. He wasn't a house pet, but at least she'd have more time to find a suitable home for him. And he wouldn't be alone for Christmas.

Alice was about to leave, but Louise was already walking toward the lone cat who remained at the facility.

"It can't hurt to take a look at it," Louise said, following the attendant to the area with the cat cages.

"Now how could anyone desert you?" Louise asked, peering into the one occupied cage. "We'd better take this one home too."

As surprised as she was, Alice was elated too. No pet would linger at the shelter this Christmas.

The young man was quick to find a carrier for the cat, and he willingly took it to the car when Louise lifted it and found it too heavy to easily move.

Jane was astonished to see them return with a dog and a cat, but she quickly set about making a bed for the sheltie in the mudroom.

"We really can't give him the run of the inn, can we?" she asked.

Alice had to agree, but she could lavish attention on him regardless of where he was.

"We should give him a name," she suggested.

"Something biblical," Jane suggested.

Louise laughed as loud as Alice. "I'm afraid the scamp is more holy terror than holy. Let's call him Job, because he suffered the longest at the shelter. And I suspect he'll make us suffer a bit too before he gets a permanent home."

"You don't mind if he stays until then?" Alice asked in surprise.

"If there's one thing Christmas has taught us, it's to welcome strangers into our midst," Louise said thoughtfully. "I think Job and I will become good friends."

The Christmas Eve service seemed especially beautiful that year. Alice sat with her sisters in their favorite pew, and the familiar conclusion brought tears to her eyes. Two candles were lit at the altar, and the light was passed down every row in the otherwise dark church. The congregation softly sang "Silent Night" while people held their little candles with paper holders to catch the drips.

"It was a lovely service," Jane said as they walked the short distance to the inn in gently falling snow.

"All that was missing was Father's sermon," Alice said, "but as long as he's in our hearts, he'll be here with us."

Jane had prepared a traditional buffet to enjoy after the service, and back at the inn they helped themselves to shrimp, cheese squares, fancy crackers, and an assortment of Christmas cookies. Afterward they gathered around the tree in the parlor to softly sing their favorite carols.

Much to Alice's surprise, Louise held the lazy old cat on her lap, stroking its head and murmuring to it between carols. Wendell lay at her feet, apparently happy with his new catnip toy and not inclined to resent the newcomer. Even more surprising, Job bounded up to her, released from the mudroom by her older sister, who smiled serenely from her favorite rocker.

"Here, boy," Alice said, getting down on the floor to lavish affection on the exuberant sheltie.

The phone rang, rather startling them since they didn't expect calls on Christmas Eve. Alice hurried to answer in the library with Job at her heels.

"I shouldn't be calling you now, but I was too excited to wait," Nia Komonos said. "I'm in Potterston staying with a friend. She has a great aunt who recently lost her beloved cat. She'd love another one but doesn't think she has the energy to take a kitten. Do you have an older cat left to adopt?"

"We do!" Alice exclaimed. "It's sitting on Louise's lap right now."

"Well, please don't give it to anyone else," Nia said. "My friend's great aunt will be thrilled to have it."

The librarian hung up, promising to call Alice as soon as she got home after Christmas.

"Good news," Alice said, rejoining her sisters. "Nia has a home for the shelter's last cat."

If Louise was disappointed not to keep it herself, she put on a good face. "I guess it's not realistic to have two cats in the inn," she said wistfully. "But this pudgy cat is certainly relaxing."

"Something feels right about sharing Christmas Eve with animals," Jane said.

"Maybe because our Lord was born in a manger in a stable for animals," Alice said thoughtfully. She sat down beside Job and petted his well-shaped head, rewarded by the thudding of his tail on the carpet. "Would it be so terrible if no one else wanted our sheltie?"

Jane shook her head, and Louise looked a bit dubious, but neither objected.

"We'd have to fence in a play area for him, of course," Alice said. "And get a nice doghouse. He's never going to be a house pet."

Still her sisters didn't object, and Alice was daydreaming about the pleasures of Job's company when they could hear the phone ringing again.

"I'll get it," Jane said. "You two enjoy your animals."

Louise was humming to the purring cat, and Alice was wondering at how calm Job was under his gentle petting.

"It's for you, Alice," Jane said, coming back with a grin on her face.

There was only one person likely to phone on Christmas Eve, and Alice hurried to take the call in the library.

"Merry Christmas," Mark said, his mellow voice completing her happiness.

"I didn't expect you to call tonight, but I'm glad you did. I have good news. All the animals have new homes except for the sheltie. I think maybe I'll be able to keep him myself."

"Then you might not want to hear my news," he said in a serious voice.

"About the sheltie?" She was torn between wanting to hear he'd found a good home and wanting to keep Job.

"I'm at the zoo—a problem with one of the kangaroos. I was talking to a night custodian who also farms. He has teenage kids, and their border collie recently passed away. A Shetland sheepdog is the perfect replacement, since they have some sheep to look after. He's excited to adopt one."

"Oh." It was all Alice could say.

"I could tell him it's not available anymore," Mark suggested kindly.

"No, Job—that's what we're calling him—belongs in the country where he has space to run. I guess it wouldn't be a good life for him penned up in town."

"I'm sorry," Mark said. "Not for finding him a home, but because you had your heart set on keeping him. I'm proud of you for considering the dog's welfare."

"This means every animal in the shelter has a home for Christmas," Alice said, trying to sound cheerful.

"Thanks to your kind heart and all your work," Mark said.

"And yours. What did I do before I had you in my life?"

"You mean everything to me," Mark said. "Merry Christmas, Alice."

She went back to the parlor feeling misty eyed but deeply happy.

"Mark has a home for Job," she announced.

Louise put the pudgy cat on the floor and hugged her sister.

"I'll miss him," Alice said, "but just imagine, every pet in the shelter has a chance at a good home. I couldn't ask for a better Christmas gift."

Alice wiped away an errant tear with the back of her hand and smiled at her beloved sisters. "And we still have Wendell."

The king of the inn came up to Alice and rubbed against her leg until she picked him up.

"Every pet deserves a loving home," Alice mused as she cuddled the cat. "But it's not just the animals who benefit. Think of all the joy Wendell brings into our lives. There's nothing more relaxing than holding him after a hard day."

She laughed with her sisters when he purred to agree with her.

I remember hearing about your adopt-a-dog idea, but I hadn't realized all that went on. Thank you for sharing it, Aunt Alice," Cynthia said. "That would make a lovely children's storybook."

They had finished opening all the gifts under the tree, and the living room floor was littered with bright, shiny papers, tissue paper, and ribbons. Wendell had descended from his footstool and was attacking the scraps of paper. He had a ribbon twisted around his neck and paw.

"Oh, Wendell. Didn't you get your present yet?" Alice took a tissue-wrapped package down from the top of a whatnot shelf where he couldn't reach it. "Here you go." She set it down for the cat. He eyed it for a moment, then pounced on it and tore into the paper. Watching his antics made them all laugh. He pulled out a fuzzy mouse with a long tail, caught it in his mouth, then tossed his head and sent it flying. Then he raced after it and pounced again.

"He does love presents," Jane said. "I'll get a trash bag. We just have time to clean this up before church." She hopped up and hurried out of the room.

They had the living room restored to order in a few moments. Each of them went to gather up purses, gloves and coats, and they met at the back door.

As they started up the path that connected Grace Chapel Inn with Grace Chapel, the church bells rang out the call to them to worship. The clear tones seemed to hang in the frost-laden air.

Jane took a deep breath and blew it out, making a cloud in the air in front of her. She looked over at her family and laughed with delight. "What a wonderful Christmas. I'd still like to know who put baby Jesus in the manger, though. Are you sure it wasn't one of you?"

Each of them denied doing it.

"Maybe it was Wendell," Cynthia said, grinning. "He's a very smart cat."

"He's a rascal, but he isn't that talented," Louise said. "Besides, he wouldn't have put it in the manger, he'd have hidden the baby where we'd never find it. Now there's another great children's story for you. The cat that stole the baby Jesus."

"Well if it wasn't any of you, and it wasn't Wendell, then who?" Alice said.

"Perhaps we had an invisible visitor last night," Jane said, raising one of her eyebrows the way Louise did. "Not that I believe in ghosts, but I imagine Mother and Father would be pleased, seeing that we still hold dear the traditions they loved."

"I'm glad you've kept the old traditions alive," Cynthia said. "It makes me feel close to Grandfather and Dad, even though they are gone, and I feel like I knew Grandmother because of all the traditions she started."

"Personally, I think an angel put Jesus in the manger," Jane said. "I like that idea."

"Your angel?" Alice said. "The one who protected you in the living Nativity?"

"You never know," Jane said, grinning. "Anything is possible at Christmas."

They all laughed, but then they fell silent, each of them considering the possibilities as they walked up the path to Grace Chapel to celebrate the birth of the Miracle-Giver.

About the Authors

*S*unni Jeffers lives in northeast Washington. She and her husband live on a farm with an aging Scottish Highlander cow and an elderly Arabian racehorse. Sunni has won the Romance Writers of America Golden Heart, American Christian Writers Book of the Year and the Colorado Romance Writer's Award of Excellence.

*P*am Hanson and Barbara Andrews are a daughter-mother writing team. They have had nearly thirty books published together, including several for Guideposts in the series Tales from Grace Chapel Inn. Pam's background is in journalism, and she previously taught at the university level for fifteen years. She and her college professor husband have two sons. Reading is her favorite pastime, and she enjoys being a volunteer youth leader at her church. Pam writes about faith and family at http://pamshanson .blogspot.com. Previous to their partnership, Barbara had twenty-one novels published under her own name. She began her career by writing Sunday school stories and contributing to antiques publications. Currently, she writes a column and articles about collectible postcards. She is the mother of four and the grandmother of eight. Barbara makes her home with Pam and her family in Nebraska.

Everyone in Acorn Hill has a favorite
Christmas breakfast recipe. Here are a couple
for you to try at home.

Jane's Monte Cristo Breakfast Strata

1 large loaf French bread (prepared ahead)

8 large eggs

2 cups whole milk (can use 2 percent milk)

1 cup cream or half-and-half

2 teaspoons Dijon mustard

1–2 teaspoons salt (preferably coarse sea salt)

2 teaspoons coarse ground pepper

4 tablespoons melted butter

3 tablespoons seedless raspberry or strawberry jam

8 ounces deli sliced ham

8 ounces deli sliced turkey breast (optional)

3 cups shredded Havarti cheese (or mild Swiss cheese)

Powdered sugar

Maple syrup

Remove crust from French bread. (Crust can be left on, if preferred.) Slice one-third of the loaf thinly. Cut the rest of the loaf into one-inch cubes. Set aside to dry out for at least an hour.

Beat together eggs, milk, cream, mustard, salt and pepper in a bowl until creamy. Blend in melted butter.

Spread jam on thin slices of bread. Cut ham and turkey breast lengthwise and crosswise into one-inch pieces. Keep separated.

Grease bottom of 9 × 13 × 2-inch baking dish. Layer ingredients: Half of the bread cubes. Layer ham over the bread. Arrange the jam-spread pieces of bread on top of ham. Spread half of the cheese over the bread. (The rest of the cheese will go on during baking.) Add a layer of turkey breast slices (optional). Top with the remaining bread cubes. (You may not need them all.)

Pour the egg mixture evenly over the layers. Cover with aluminum foil and refrigerate at least two hours or overnight.

In the morning, one and a half hours before breakfast, take strata out of refrigerator. Leave covered and place in cold oven. Turn on oven to 350 degrees. When oven reaches full temperature, bake for thirty minutes covered. Uncover and sprinkle with remaining cheese. Continue baking for twenty to forty minutes or until middle is set.

Let sit fifteen minutes. Dust lightly with powdered sugar. Cut and serve hot. Serve warm maple syrup on the side. Serves ten to twelve.

Madeleine's Salted Caramel Praline Breakfast Bread (Monkey Bread)

Biscuits:

>   3 cups flour
>
>   2 tablespoons sugar
>
>   4 teaspoons baking powder
>
>   1 teaspoon baking soda
>
>   1 teaspoon salt
>
>   1 stick butter
>
>   1 cup buttermilk (or milk with 1 teaspoon lemon juice or white vinegar; let sit for a few minutes to curdle)

Mix dry ingredients in a large bowl. Cut butter in small pieces, and cut into dry ingredients with pastry cutter or rub with fingers until coarse meal is formed. Add buttermilk and mix, and then form into ball. If batter is sticky, flour your hands. Knead lightly. Divide dough in thirds and cover each portion with plastic wrap or waxed paper to keep it from drying out.

>   Preheat oven to 350 degrees.

Topping:

>   1 stick (¼ pound) butter
>
>   1 cup light brown sugar (packed)
>
>   1 teaspoon cinnamon
>
>   ¼ teaspoon nutmeg
>
>   1 cup heavy cream or half-and-half

1 teaspoon coarse salt (preferably sea salt or kosher salt)
1 teaspoon vanilla
1 cup chopped pecans (set aside)
¼ cup sugar (set aside)
1 teaspoon cinnamon (set aside)

In saucepan, melt butter, add sugar, cinnamon and nutmeg, and stir until mixture just comes to a simmer. Add cream. Stirring constantly, bring to a boil. Remove from heat. Stir in salt and vanilla.

To assemble, grease a Bundt pan. Sprinkle bottom with one-fourth of the pecans.

In a shallow dish, blend sugar and cinnamon. Pinch off walnut-size pieces of biscuit dough and roll in cinnamon-sugar mixture. Place loosely in bottom of Bundt pan, using one-third of the biscuit dough. Drizzle with one-third of the caramel sauce and sprinkle with one-fourth of the pecans. Repeat for two more layers.

Bake at 350 degrees for thirty-five to forty minutes. While still hot, invert onto large round plate, like a cake plate. Best served warm. Break off in pieces to serve. Serves ten to twelve.

A Note from the Editors

We hope you enjoy Tales from Grace Chapel Inn, created by the Books and Inspirational Media Division of Guideposts. In all of our books, magazines and outreach efforts, we aim to deliver inspiration and encouragement, help you grow in your faith, and celebrate God's love in every aspect of your daily life.

Thank you for making a difference with your purchase of this book, which helps fund our many outreach programs to the military, prisons, hospitals, nursing homes and schools. To learn more, visit GuidepostsFoundation.org.

We also maintain many useful and uplifting online resources. Visit Guideposts.org to read true stories of hope and inspiration, access OurPrayer network, sign up for free newsletters, join our Facebook community, and follow our stimulating blogs. For more articles to get you into the true spirit of Christmas, visit Guideposts.org/Christmas.

To order your favorite Guideposts publications, go to ShopGuideposts.org, call (800) 932-2145 or write to Guideposts, PO Box 5815, Harlan, Iowa 51593.